SUMMER
OF THE
WOLVES

SUMMER
OF THE
WOLVES

by Polly Carlson-Voiles

🐦 sandpiper

HOUGHTON MIFFLIN HARCOURT
Boston New York

SANDPIPER and the SANDPIPER logo are trademarks of Houghton
Mifflin Harcourt Publishing Company.

For information about permission to reproduce selections from this
book, write to Permissions, Houghton Mifflin Harcourt Publishing
Company, 215 Park Avenue South, New York, New York 10003.

www.hmhco.com

The text of this book is set in Dante.

The Library of Congress has cataloged the hardcover edition as follows:
Carlson-Voiles, Polly, 1943–.
Summer of the wolves / by Polly Carlson-Voiles.
p. cm.
[1. Wolves—Fiction. 2. Orphans—Fiction. 3. Wilderness areas—Fiction.
4. Minnesota—Fiction.] I. Title.
PZ7. C21682Su 2012
[Fic]—dc23
2011039909

ISBN: 978-0-547-74591-6 hardcover
ISBN: 978-0-544-02276-8 paperback

Manufactured in the United States of America
DOC 10 9 8 7 6 5 4 3 2

4500473768

To my partner, husband, patient reader, and best friend, Steve Voiles, whose love and support have meant so much during the writing of this book. To the precious natural places and wild creatures of the world. And to the young people who seek to learn about and love wilderness and its many gifts.

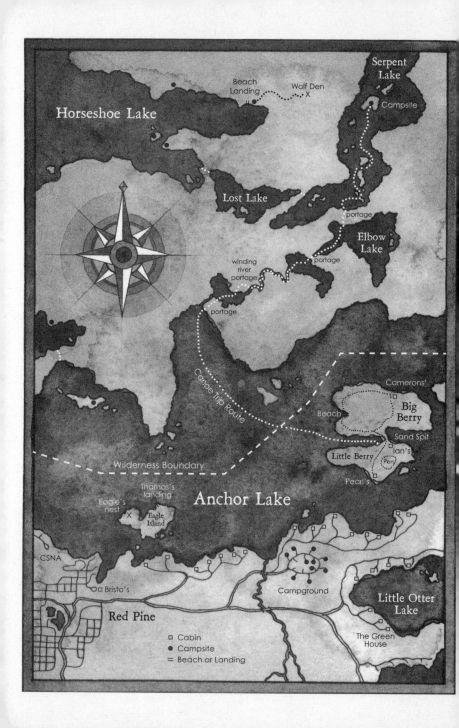

Birds make great sky-circles of their freedom.

How do they learn it?

They fall, and falling, they are given wings.

—*Rumi*

When the earth-colored wolf pup first opened her eyes, she looked into the eyes of a woman. The woman's voice was gentle; her hands were strong. The pup couldn't remember her lost pack mates or being pulled from the collapsed den. In the first weeks of the pup's life, the woman fed her from bottles and slept beside her on layers of clean straw spread on the floor of an old wooden shed.

Chapter One

As she walked home from school that perfect California spring day, Nika felt she was on solid ground for the first time in nineteen months, two weeks, and five days. The constant changes for her and her brother had been like Alice down the rabbit hole, a book Nika had never been fond of. You'd have to be in a pretty steady spot in the world to love a book like that.

For Nika, being orphaned at ten and a half had been like standing on a major fault line during an earthquake, watching land slide away in every direction. She'd held tight to her brother's hand and tried to stay on her feet. Being alone was the new normal, but the shaking never completely stopped. Now the shock was to wake up and find she could do something ordinary like go down for breakfast and shout at her brother for spilling on her English essay, then go off to school like everyone else her age. Nika knew that some animals just plain die when they lose a parent. They give up. It was easy to understand how that could happen.

But today was a good day. After school she walked Olivia home and made plans to get together later. Nika ambled along the streets of Pasadena in the flowery air of April. In her backpack she had test scores that would make any parent proud. If she'd had a parent, that is. Well, Meg would be proud. Red-purple bougainvillea vines massed up the sides of small houses, and she felt the neon color at the backs of her eyes. A rare sense of peace and exhilaration washed over her, and she stopped smack in the middle of the sidewalk to savor the moment. She had her best friends, Olivia and Zack. School was tolerable since the clone-girls with matching outfits and hairstyles had stopped snickering at her behind their hands. Meg was a great foster mom. Life was finally okay, under the circumstances.

On the corner of her street Nika stopped as usual to speak to Rookie, a bear-size St. Bernard / Great Pyrenees cross, one of the dogs she walked after school for extra money. He had stolen her heart with his droolly, golden-hearted loving ways. Every day he waited for her, leaning against the gate where she could reach over and rub his ears. She could always tell Rookie about how much she missed her mom, or about the girls who teased her for being too smart. Things she never told anyone else.

When she looked into his heavy-lidded knowing eyes, she remembered how she and Randall had bombarded their mom with dog-acquiring campaigns: hidden notes, pictures, and impossible promises. Their mom would always laugh and say, "Someday . . ."

She rubbed the dog's chest until he collapsed into a giant furry puddle, then knelt down to scratch him through the fence. Dogs love you no matter what.

"Someday . . ." she said softly to the dog, as she rose to walk up the street to Meg's. She had homework to do if she was going to go back to Olivia's later.

When she got home, the house echoed with tiptoe quiet. She found a note under the frog magnet on the fridge that said, "The twins and Josie are with their social workers. Randall is at a game with Newt. I am grocery shopping. Be back soon. Luv, Meg." There was a heart drawn by the signature.

Nika threw her quarter-ton book bag onto the couch, poured some milk, grabbed an apple, and pulled out her math homework, settling in for a bout with pre-algebra. Two minutes on the soft couch in the silent house, and she fell asleep with the book unopened in her hands.

o o o

A shrill ringing spiked into Nika's sleep, vibrating inside her head like a dentist's drill. She threw herself sideways off the couch, jumped up, and grabbed the phone before it could ring again.

"Hello," she answered, trying to focus, her heart beating fast from sudden awakening.

"Hello. Is this Nika?" said an unfamiliar nervous-chirpy voice.

"Yes, speaking."

"Well, this is Mrs. Marquita Fish. You remember? Your Pasadena social worker? I have recently been talking to Meg, uh, to your foster mother, and I wanted you both to know the good news right away. Please, would you call Meg to the phone?"

Good news? Good news coming from this social worker? The very one who moved Nika and her brother to a new foster home every two months before placing them at Meg's eleven months ago? At the last foster home before Meg's, the woman in charge had kept the shades drawn and never let anyone open a window, even if it was hot, and an older boy had thrown Nika's pet turtle over the fence. *I can hardly wait,* she thought. But politeness reigned, manners her mother had taught her. "She's not home right now. May I take a message?"

"Yes, well . . ." said Mrs. Fish. There was a questioning silence on the line. "So then, Nika, when do you think Meg will be available?"

Nika always stumbled when she tried to lie. Pausing, she said, "She's coming home late, I think. Really, really late." Something about this call made her want to curl her toes into the nubby tan carpet and hold on.

Suddenly Mrs. Fish spoke more loudly, like people do to the hard of hearing. "Yes, well, I guess I'll tell you the good news first. We've finally found your uncle. He'd been out of the country. But we've found him, and it's all arranged!" She ended on a high note, as though she had just announced winning a free car on the radio.

"What?" Nika's jumpy feet began propelling her back and forth. *Arranged? Uncle???* Her finger lingered on the phone's "end call" button. Her only uncle had been out of the picture for years.

"Oh, nooooo. I guess Meg hasn't told you yet. Oh, my. I've probably spoiled the surprise. You and Randall are going to Minnesota!" High note again. "Your uncle bought the tickets. It's all set. Week after next!"

Nika wanted to swat at the woman's voice to make it stop. Instead she took a breath and held it. Pushing her words tight together so there wouldn't be room for Mrs. Fish to say more, Nika said, "There must be some mistake because school isn't over for weeks, but thanks." She abruptly pushed the "end call" button. Meg could call her back. Or not. Nika could just forget to mention it. She felt a hot tightening in her stomach. A visit to Minnesota the week after next, before school was even out? Impossible. She was just getting used to living in a foster home she liked. Surely Meg would let Nika and Randall decide.

During the next hour Nika paced so much, she practically wore a pathway in the carpet. Finally Meg struggled in through the back door, breathing heavily, her bag of groceries catching on the doorjamb. Nika rushed to help her with the tearing bag.

She hadn't planned to tell Meg. Especially since she knew Meg hadn't been feeling well lately. But for Nika honesty sometimes just happened, like when your hand shoots out as you're about to fall. Before she had time to stop herself, she said, "Mrs. Fish called about some uncle." Nika lifted the torn bag carefully and heaved it to the counter. Several cans and boxes tumbled out.

Meg gave her a long look while straightening her flowered shirt. They stood staring at each other in the sunny kitchen. It felt as if out of nowhere a dangerous snake had entered the room. The clock in the kitchen ticked out the beats of her heart.

"Something . . . about Minnesota, I think," Nika said, lowering the volume of her voice to near zero.

This was silly, she thought. She already knew what Meg was going to say with a laugh. She would say, *You know you are welcome to stay here as long as you want!*

But instead, in halting tones, her foster mother said, "Oh, I'm so sorry. I'm glad she called. But . . . you should have heard it first from me." After a stiff moment she turned away, then looked back at Nika. No usual smiles. Her foster mom looked sad, as if she was trying not to cry. Nika felt dizzy.

Meg wrapped her in a gentle hug. "Nika, you know I love you and Randall." Her voice quivered. Then she let go and folded into a kitchen chair. "And honestly, I would have kept you as long as you needed to stay."

Would have? Tendrils of dread crept up Nika's body from her toes. There was something *else* Meg hadn't told her.

"Would have?" Nika asked. A knot was building in her throat.

"Yes, I would have. But I can't. Some problems have developed with my heart. I've been trying to find a way to tell you. I'm scheduled to go into the hospital for some tests. The doctor wants me to give up fostering for a while and to devote myself entirely to getting well. Mrs. Fish found places right away for the younger ones, but I have been so worried about you and Randall, after all you've been through. So Mrs. Fish agreed to try again to locate your father's brother."

Again? Contact him *again?* Right. Nika needed to act. As with the mudslides last spring in the canyon up behind Pasadena, once again she felt as if a whole hill were moving and there was no place to grab hold. "I know. I've got an idea," she said quickly with a fake strong voice. "Let's just figure out a way to stay here in Pasadena with someone else." She took a breath. "Maybe Olivia's? They've got an extra room since her sister went to college. I can walk more dogs and take care of people's cats when they go away. Then after you're better, we'll come back. We could even come over and cook for you, bring magazines and stuff. You know I can clean, and I know which days are for garbage and recycling."

Meg's face crumpled. The woman Nika had grown to love was upbeat and strong. Now here she was, bent in a chair, speaking with a thick, defeated voice. "Oh, Nika, honey, I'm so sorry. I was hoping your uncle would travel here . . ." She paused, shook her head, and then said, "Oh, this is all so hard, but I'm afraid the plans are made. I was just waiting to hear back from Mrs. Fish." She stood and reached out to Nika.

At first Nika stood with her arms clutched in front of her, but who else would comfort her? The two of them collapsed together in a hug. After they had a good cry, Meg reached for the teakettle. She made blueberry tea, and they each had a cup, sitting in the yellow kitchen with the groceries still in bags.

By the time Randall got home, Nika felt light and sharp and closed. Now even Meg couldn't fill the emptiness where family should have been.

In a special babysitting class Nika had taken this year they'd studied child development. The textbook said most of what you learn happens in the early years. So, she figured, however she'd turned out at twelve, she was done, like a baked cake. Randall was only seven. Maybe he was still young enough to want a parent who held the bike seat while he learned to ride. But she didn't need a new family. She'd had a great mom. Meg's had been a loving hand to hold. End of story. She would be the girl in the Brave Girl Movie and take care of herself and Randall. If they had to go to another foster home in Pasadena, she could handle it.

But no way was she leaving California for good. Since Mom had moved them across the country, they hadn't even visited Minnesota. Mrs. Fish obsessed about the idea of real blood relatives and must have put out an all points bulletin. If Nika and Randall had to, they would visit this missing-in-action uncle. That was all.

From that phone call on, the days ran together like smearing paint. Saying goodbyes. Packing. Gathering make-up assignments from her teachers. After what happened last year, she wouldn't miss the clone-girls very much, but Olivia and Zack were her friends forever. How would she live without her best friends for six whole weeks? She and Olivia cried and laughed together during one last sleepover. They traded necklaces they made for each other, then said goodbye, promising to write real handwritten letters, stamped and sent through the mail.

Nika spent an extra-long time with Rookie the day before she left. His owner, Glenna, invited her in for a Coke and cookies. Rookie leaned against Nika's leg the entire time, and she wrapped her arms around his immense neck. She thought he looked sad. Maybe he was picking up her feelings. She knew dogs can do that.

When May tenth finally came and they lined up for security in the L.A. airport, Nika hugged Meg so hard, they both stopped breathing for a moment. Over and over Nika kept reassuring herself. *Whatever happens, this is just a visit. In a few weeks it will be over. We are coming back. If Meg gets better, we can maybe even live with her again.*

As the wolf became an adult, her coat grew in silvery-tan with pale gray markings. Her golden eyes followed every movement outside her fence. The woman visited with food, sometimes bringing road-killed deer. In the woman's absence the wolf stood watching, her ears forward in attention. Most days she paced the boundaries of the fence, or danced below the raven that taunted her from his perch of freedom. From beyond the fence came unknown smells. Sometimes she heard howling in the night and howled back. With her large paws she dug holes in the ground by the buried fence, holes the woman soon filled with rocks.

Chapter Two

A Minnesota social worker with downcast eyes and a one-sided smile met Nika and Randall at the Minneapolis air terminal. The attendant from the airlines checked identities and paperwork, and they were handed over like two packages, postage paid. During the long walk from the landing gate, the social worker moved them along almost at a trot, introducing herself in hurried breaths as Ms. Vera Nordstrom. In the drizzly airport parking lot, she loaded them into her maroon minivan, giving them nervous, hurried smiles.

On the interstate, Ms. Nordstrom followed a map marked with a yellow line, staying in the slow lane. Her windshield wipers flapped for the first hour and very few words were spoken. Through the window Nika saw cars and big parking lots and dull gray buildings at first, then gradually more trees and farms as they got farther from the city. They stopped at a rest stop with bathrooms and soda pop machines, then once more for Mexican fast food. Randall fidgeted in the seat belt beside her, tearing the wrapper from his burrito until small pieces littered the seat. When Nika stared at his mess and raised her eyebrows, he just half smiled and shrugged.

Just as the sun began to win the battle with the clouds, the van left the highway and nosed down several unmarked dirt roads, arriving at the starred location on the map. It didn't look promising, just a steep gravel drive, a small rusted shed, and a large gray wooden dock perched at the edge of a long narrow lake.

Randall and Nika huddled on the dock with their small cluster of bags. Ms. Nordstrom loomed behind them, a sheepdog in position. It was cooler than Pasadena but not as cool as Nika had expected. The air smelled like Christmas tree needles. Long bands of sunlight laced through the tall trees. Occasional bird songs fluted over the water. Nika began to take mental snapshots: puddles on the ground reflecting sky, broken branches strewn beside the dock. She wondered if there had been a recent storm. The forest around them was dotted with a million neon-green buds on curtains of bare branches. Darker green trees with needles were everywhere. Of course, there wasn't a palm or cactus in sight.

Then, on the lake's far side, a plane dropped out of the sky like an insect, almost soundless as it flew. When it hit the water, they heard the distant hum of its motor. Randall slowly walked to the very end of the dock, his eyes fixed on the plane.

Ms. Nordstrom moved closer to Nika. "Imagine the children who never get an opportunity like this. You are so lucky. Oh, I know how hard this has been, at your age, such *incredible* loss . . ." Her words were like picking at a scab that was almost healed. Always, always, there was that picture in her head of her mom climbing into her friend Barb's car, her mom smiling and waving.

Nika jerked in a breath and looked away from the woman. An awkward silence spread around them like rings in a pool. Then the low mosquito buzz swelled to a small roar as the plane approached.

Ms. Nordstrom leaned toward Nika, shot her gaze at Randall, and shout-whispered over the noise of the plane, "Well. Even if you don't want to be here, think about Randall." She crossed her arms.

Nika bit back a rude response. What she didn't need was some strange social worker telling her about Randall's feelings. During the days preparing for this visit, she'd watched Randall's excitement mushroom as he gathered his fishing gear and looked at maps.

She was relieved when the wall of noise and wind from the plane stopped further conversation. Then the engine cut to sudden silence, and a bright yellow float-plane drifted in to thump against the rubber tire bumpers on the dock. A man hopped out onto the float, then onto the dock. His face was framed by dark curling hair, his eyes crinkled above a smiley opening in his beard. "Hi. I'm Reino Makinen," he said. "Ian McNeill's pilot." He effortlessly looped ropes around posts to tie the plane. "Good old Finnish name. Everyone calls me Maki."

Why hadn't their uncle come along to pick them up? Nika looked at the plane—it seemed so small. *Some uncle,* she thought, *asking us to risk our lives, flying in this thing.*

Looking at their lumpy duffel bags and backpacks on the dock, Maki said, "This everything?"

"Yeah," Nika answered, looking over their pathetic pile. "Pretty much."

Nothing could have been truer. Except for some stuff they'd left in storage back at Meg's, everything important they owned was inside those sad heaps of nylon. Socks, CD players, CDs, a copy of *Just So Stories,* and report cards. Some photographs, Meg's address, old jeans, friends' school pictures, toothbrushes, and Band-Aids. Randall's superhero cards, Nika's old brown bear, sweatshirts with their school motto, records of vaccinations,

Nika's journal. There was the stuff her uncle had had them buy at a camping store—bug repellent, new hiking boots that laced up above the ankle, hats, pants, and hooded jackets called anoraks, the clothes still bearing tags.

Nika pulled her worn orange backpack from the heap.

Maki smoothly loaded the rest into the back of the plane, then said, "Well then, let's fly. How about it?"

They said a quick goodbye to Ms. Nordstrom, unsuccessful at dodging the stiff hugs she gave them.

With the hug, Ms. Nordstrom couldn't resist a few last words to Nika, very close to her ear: "It's up to the oldest to set the proper tone. I hope you're going to do your best to make this placement work!"

Placement. As if she and Randall were merchandise about to be positioned on a newly dusted shelf.

They settled into the back seat, and the plane began to pull slowly away from the dock. Nika looked into the empty front seat, to the right of Maki. There was a second pretzel-shaped control that moved when Maki turned his steering wheel. As if a ghost were flying in the right seat. As the plane tugged against the water, she remembered one important question she'd forgotten to ask. She'd meant to ask Ms. Nordstrom what excuse this Wonder Uncle had given her for his being so completely gone from their lives, for not even showing up for their mom's funeral, for being gone during a time when everything in their world had turned upside down, inside out, and backwards.

Nika's teeth knocked together as the small plane erupted into a blast of sound during takeoff. She gripped her backpack as they became airborne and the roar settled into a loud, vibrating drone. When they tipped into a turn, it felt as if the lake were falling away. She smiled at Randall to show him she wasn't scared, even though she was. But Randall seemed unaffected, hunched at his window, his forehead pressed against the glass. When the plane straightened out, Nika leaned and watched until Ms. Nordstrom and her minivan became dots on the lakeshore and finally disappeared from sight.

Beneath them now was a rug of trees stitched through with threads of rivers and patched with lakes. An occasional ribbon of road led to a miniature house. As they sailed above, Nika settled into the monotone of engine sound. The smell of oil and scorched metal reminded her of the service garage near Meg's house.

Randall seemed hypnotized by the view. "Wow, can you believe it? It's nothing but trees down there. Like an ocean." He smiled at Nika and settled back in his seat.

Maki handed Randall and Nika large headphones.

When she fitted them over her ears, she didn't like how the engine noise seemed distant and unreal, as if they were in a tunnel at the water park.

After about ten muffled minutes, Nika released the death grip she had on her backpack, dug around, pulled out her yellow journal, and flipped to the back, where she'd made a taped-on pocket. It held three letters. She picked up the one that had arrived soon after Mrs. Fish's call. The letter was tattered from being unfolded and refolded by Randall.

Dear Annika and Randall,

I couldn't believe it when I opened my mail and found the letter from Mrs. Fish. Yes, I am your father's brother. He was much younger and we weren't really close. I'm sorry that after he died I lost track of your family.

I was distressed to hear about your mom. I wish I had known. Apparently your mom's accident happened when I was in Finland and Russia studying wolves. The letter written to inform me must have gotten lost.

I live way up in northern Minnesota now, almost on the Canadian border, where I do wildlife research with wolves. I hope you don't mind the timing, but it seemed best for you to start your visit before I get busy with the summer season.

Anyway, I will try to call when I can get into town. (Cell phones never work here on the island.) I look forward to your visit.

Your uncle, Ian McNeill

The thing about cell phones not working where Ian lived was a plus. All of her friends with real families had unlimited text messaging, and being a foster child, she had never been able to afford a cell phone. Visiting the hinterlands, she wouldn't be the odd girl out.

Nika remembered how when they first got this letter, Randall had slipped onto the edge of her chair and asked her to read it again. She had felt his shoulders lift as he took a breath and held it.

"He studies wolves, Nika, real wolves," he'd said. She had to admit that was pretty interesting but no excuse for losing track of two human children. "And he has the same last name," Randall added.

She and Randall had sat together and written a letter back, using a stamp from Randall's collection that had a picture of a cat. Nika found the copy that Mrs. Fish made of that letter with the others.

Dear Ian McNeill,

Randall and I would like to come visit for a few weeks. We are used to being helpful around the house, and we won't cause any trouble. Right now we're staying at a pretty neat foster home, and we hope to come back here later.

It's okay if you are not around all of the time because I am used to looking after Randall anyway and we have been taught to be responsible and not do things we are not supposed to do.

Sincerely, Annika and Randall McNeill

When Nika read this letter back to Randall, he'd given her a thumbs-up, a sliver of his old full-moon smile beginning to rise, his eyes never leaving the paper in her hands.

As they flew, Nika felt for the necklace Olivia had made for her, a circle of green jade. She'd made Olivia one just like it. It calmed her to touch the coolness of the stone. Then she unfolded the third letter, also from Mystery Uncle. In this one it looked like he was already trying to unload them on somebody else.

Dear Annika and Randall,

We are all excited about your coming visit.

I'm sorry to say that my cabin on Little Berry Island is awfully small (one room), so I've made plans for Randall to stay with a really nice family on an attached island, called Big Berry Island. We've arranged for him to go to school by boat with their three boys those last weeks of school. Their cabin is close so we can visit every day and do things together.

Since Nika will have make-up credits to do and won't need to go to school, she has been invited to stay in Pearl's cabin, up the hill from me on Little Berry Island. Pearl is like a grandma to everyone. I have known her for years, I rent my cabin from her, and eat my meals with her. She's a good friend.

Looking forward to your visit,

Your uncle, Ian McNeill

Nika carefully refolded this letter and returned it to the pocket of her journal. Probably this uncle was just trying to do the right thing. Have the kids visit. Duty done. He wasn't even married. What would he want with kids?

She glanced at Randall where he sat with his head bent forward, one of his dragon books opened in his lap. Not knowing what else to do, Nika pulled her journal out again. She'd write something, like she was supposed to for English credit. She arranged the yellow journal in her lap and uncapped her pen. The vibrations of the plane made her handwriting jiggle raggedly across the page.

We are high in the air, somewhere . . . in a plane so small it's like a flying minivan. When I lean up to look out the front, I can see right through the propeller, it spins so fast. And the plane has floats for landing on the water. Flying is neat, though. Kind of like being nowhere and in between. Anything seems possible.

Suddenly Nika felt queasy as the sky pitched by, so she put her pen away. Her ears were popping. She searched in the pocket behind the front seat for the Ziploc barf bags Maki had mentioned. She'd almost forgotten how she always got sick after reading or writing in a moving vehicle.

To calm her stomach, she closed her eyes. When she opened them again, nothing much had changed. The sky was clear-water blue. The plane's shadow flickered over a toy town that looked like a half-done jigsaw puzzle.

When she cast a look at Randall again, he had fallen

asleep, one hand holding on to the strap of his backpack, his dragon book beside him on the seat. Seeing him like that, a little drool rolling down his chin and his dark blond hair sweaty and standing up on one side, made her think of the bus bench by Meg's house. Large red letters were printed on the backrest announcing, "ADOPT SIBLINGS—sometimes all they have is each other."

Nika removed the muffling headphones and settled into the thunderous rhythm of the engine. After an hour of steady flying, Maki suddenly leaned to the side and looked out his window. Turning to Nika and Randall and waving for their attention, he shouted, "Look off to the left! See that bare hill surrounded by trees? Five wolves are down there taking a rest!"

All she could see on the hill below were some small gray rocks. She poked Randall to wake him up.

"I'll circle down closer," Maki said, pulling the plane into a steep turn.

In a pileup at the window, Nika and Randall stared through a full turn of the sky as the plane swept down closer to the ground. It felt as if they might fall right out of the plane. Finally, they could see that what had looked like rocks was a pack of wolves stretched out like dogs napping in the yard. With Nika's head on Randall's shoulder, they leaned to watch until the wolves were finally out of sight.

"Wow," Randall said. "Just like the Discovery Channel!"

One had been black, Nika noticed. She never knew that wolves could be black as well as gray. She pulled out her journal to write about the black wolf. But before she could write three words, she felt a metal taste in her mouth. She salivated and swallowed hard. This was not a good sign. She looked around for the bag.

"How much farther?" she asked.

"Ten minutes or so," Maki answered.

For a while she felt better. But then the plane began to tilt again and slip dizzyingly through the air. Her head felt hot, and her stomach clambered up toward her shoulders, as if it weren't planning to go along with the rest of her body as they headed down. She pulled out the bag and opened it. As Maki managed the pretzel-shaped control, he flashed a smile in their direction as though, for him, this were a swan ride at the kiddie park. With a slight move, he tipped the plane into a steeper angle.

That's when she threw up, her face in the bag. Randall looked at her and plugged his nose. "Yuck," he said. Nika perspired, gasped, and swallowed. How embarrassing. All she wanted was a breath of fresh air, anything but the burned metal and oil smell of the plane. She threw up again.

Maki looked back and raised his eyebrows. "You okay?" he asked loudly. "Almost there, hang on."

She nodded.

He pointed through the down-tilted window at two islands below them, shouting, "There they are! What we call Big Berry and Little Berry Islands. Hold tight. I've got to head down lake a bit, so I can land into the wind."

Nika raised her head to see a slim band of white sand linking the islands, as if they were holding hands.

After another circle in the air, they started to descend. A down-elevator weightlessness made Nika reach for Randall's arm and a second bag, just in case. Suddenly the plane lurched, and she slid forward into her seat belt, knocking her backpack to the floor. She peeked out to see water spraying up as land raced by at eye level. The roar intensified as the plane motored into a small bay between the arms of two islands. On both sides Nika saw rocks, water, trees.

As the plane grumbled closer, Nika noticed a man standing on a square dock squinting into the light, one hand shading his eyes. Beside him stood a smaller figure in a red shirt. The dock seemed suspended from a massive shelf of rock.

Nika slouched down in her seat and reached to drape her arm over Randall's thin shoulders. He must be scared. Glancing at the bag she was holding, he wrinkled his nose, shrugged away from her, and said, "You stink. Nothing personal."

Then she followed the direction of Randall's eyes. They were locked onto the dock and the two waiting figures.

One day in spring, the air turned soggy and warm. The wolf sought the cooling earth of her hillside den. Suddenly, like an intake of breath, there was a threatening hush. Then a scouring wind bent the trees of the forest, followed by rumbles and cracks. Rain ran in streams down the hill, flooding her den. Outside the pen, trees fell in every direction, blown like straws in the mouth of the wind. Searing light flashed, followed by earth-shaking booms.

Chapter Three

Maki killed the engine. Waves slapped the floats and rocked the plane until it thumped against the dock. Nika took in a long breath, then exhaled slowly to calm herself, as Meg had taught her. But her stomach still churned like a cement mixer. She held a hand over her mouth, not wanting to stagger from the plane and throw up on her newfound uncle's boots.

She tried to get her jelly legs to move. What would this woodsy uncle think of her city-tight mismatched clothes and her short, spiky, almost-black hair? As Ms. Nordstrom probably had done, would he take one look and think, *Uh-oh*? She raked her hand through her hair to flatten it a little.

Maki reached back, handing her a thermos. "Drink this," he said. "Swish it around a little. Then drink some more. I'll take the bag." The water made a cool path down her throat. She drank several more sips and felt better. She aimed a weak smile at Maki, who placed her Ziploc bag in a plastic garbage sack and tied it tightly. Then Maki opened the door, stepped out onto the pontoon, and tossed a couple of ropes to the man on the dock.

"Hey, Ian!" Maki shouted. "Brought your special deliveries . . . one's a little ragged from the flight!" He laughed and bent over to look inside the cabin of the plane.

Nika felt sewn into her seat. Her muscles wouldn't budge.

"Annika, move!" Randall said, suddenly impatient. She couldn't remember him ever calling her by her whole first name.

A blast of bright sunlight washed across Nika's face as Maki helped her onto the float, then onto the dock. Randall hopped out as if he did this every day. But then he lost courage and slipped behind Nika, leaning his thin seven-year-old body into her back. There was a sharp pine smell in the air, completely different from the chlorine-and-roses smell of Pasadena.

Nika reached back, pulled Randall around beside her, and whispered, "Say hi, Randall."

Looking down at his shoes, Randall said, "Yeah, hi." A megawatt smile slowly rose on his face. That was Randall—quick recovery. *Not like me,* Nika thought.

The woman in the red shirt looked strong and tanned, her gray hair short and wavy. Reaching out a hand to each of them, she stepped forward. "Pearl Guthrie. Just call me Pearl." Holding on to their hands, she said, "Aren't we lucky to have such nice weather today? The ice went out over three weeks early this year. It's almost like summer already."

In the letter Ian had called Pearl "everyone's grandma." Nika supposed that meant everyone liked her. She was slightly stooped but agile-looking, dressed in tan pants and a white T-shirt, wearing a bright red flannel shirt like a jacket. Nika liked her eyes. They were blue, like small pieces of sky, turning up at the corners in an eye-smile.

From behind Pearl, the man came forward, hands in pockets. He was dressed in khaki clothes that looked as though they might have been trampled on repeatedly by large herds of wild animals. He was tall and lean and had dark brown eyes behind rimless glasses, and his curly almost-black hair waved down over his collar. His face was tanned and clean-shaven. His whole posture had an athletic bend, as if he'd be ready to run at the drop of a hat. She could hardly blame him if he did.

After seeming to look them over, Ian reached out to Randall, shaking his hand.

Nika stood very still, trying to breathe normally, feeling her stomach continue to threaten.

Randall smiled and said, "Nika barfed . . ."

Nika jabbed him and scowled, keeping her eyes on Ian. Clutching her backpack tight in front of her, she stared at this unknown male relative.

"Well, Annika, I'm Ian McNeill. You all right?"

She nodded.

"Well, good. You can call me Ian, or Uncle Ian, or whatever." He laughed in a nervous way, shifting his feet, seeming unsure. Maybe he hadn't been around a lot of orphans. She stood very still, thinking how weird it was that this stranger had the same last name as theirs.

"Yeah, hi. Okay. Well, you can call me Nika. People only call me Annika at the dentist's office or when they're mad." Ian laughed, as if he enjoyed what she'd just said. Nika studied him.

Meg had said he was forty-two, but he looked younger. His face was serious and calm, not unfriendly, but thoughtful.

"You resemble your mother," Ian said, looking sad as he spoke. She didn't know why people said that to her. Nika had dark hair and blue eyes. Her mom had been blond with hazel eyes and looked more like Randall. Ian's mouth opened as if he were going to say something else. Thankfully, he stopped himself.

More than anything, Nika hated people talking about

what had happened to her family. It made her feel like a run-over animal lying in the street, everyone standing over her, looking down and discussing the nature of her injuries. She held her backpack tighter, locking her arms.

Like a coach trying to rally the team, Ian said, "Everybody ready? Let's take stuff up the hill. I'll show you around, and then we'll all have supper up at Pearl's. You two have had a long day." He reached out with one hand to wave Maki ahead of him, then leaned and scooped up bags, smiling shyly as he moved.

Relieved that there was no more conversation, Nika shifted her pack to her back and grabbed another bag. Loaded up, they all caravaned past a couple of boats and a screen house, then up a stretch of log steps wedged into the hillside.

At the top of the steps, a small yippy dog came skidding toward them. He circled Pearl and leaped up for a pat, then ran to sniff Nika's shoes. Randall squatted down, and the dog licked his ear, making Randall laugh. He was black with stand-up hair and stand-up ears, giving him a surprised look. Just like a smart movie dog, he cocked his head far to one side.

"Meet Zeus," laughed Pearl, throwing a stick into the bushes for him. Quickly bringing it back, he ran to the front of the line with his head high, the stick dangling from the side of his mouth.

They angled their way upward on the narrowing

path. Elbow-high bushes grabbed at Nika's shirt, and she heard the high-pitched conversations of birds above. As they climbed between the massive trunks of linebacker-size trees, the ground became more open, carpeted with reddish-brown pine needles.

Suddenly Nika stopped and looked up, causing Randall to bang into her.

"Watch out, Nika," he complained.

She'd heard a sound up high. In front of her, Pearl had stopped as well. "Wind in the tops of the pines," the older woman said. Almost like ocean surf, it came and went like breathing. The tops of the trees were so high that Nika got dizzy looking up.

Pearl said wistfully, "That sound always reminds me of home and listening to a faraway train coming across the prairie." Nika had never been on a train. Or heard one. As they started climbing again, she glanced ahead to see Pearl smile at her.

Nika's muscles began to feel the steepness. Coming out of the shade of the large trees, they climbed onto a clean skirt of rock that draped the hillside ahead of them. Nika stopped for a minute to catch her breath. Ahead, Pearl didn't even pause. The rock ledge they walked across looked melted at the edges. It was as broad as a parking lot with veins of rust-colored rock winding through. At the top stood a postcard-perfect log house with a bright red door.

Ian stood waiting for Nika and Randall to catch up. "This'll be where you'll stay, Nika," he said.

She shot a curious glance in Ian's direction as he led the way to the red painted door. She hadn't had a boatload of adult men in her life and didn't know what to expect. She kept her eyes on him as they stepped into the house. She was almost jealous watching Randall receive Ian's high-five at the doorway.

Nika felt dwarfed by the large, open living room. It was built of logs bigger around than her body. The ceiling vaulted up to roof windows throwing blocks of sunlight down onto the hardwood floor. She was grateful when Pearl came over, put her arm around Nika, and said, "Let me show you around."

Pearl's whole house was walled with logs stained a warm golden color. A deck with chairs jutted off the front next to the door, overlooking the lake. On the first floor was a huge room with deep comfortable chairs in one corner next to a bookcase and windows with small panes of glass. A table large enough for a scout troop and made from half-logs was in the center of this room. Nika noticed delicate watercolor paintings and Native American designs arranged on the walls. In the back of the first floor were two small rooms with large windows. One held a bed and dresser and paintings of birds on the walls. Pearl's room. The other had shelves and large low drawers, with a drawing table piled with paintbrushes in holders and bins of art materials. "My studio," Pearl said, smiling. Through a screened porch was a back door leading to a walkway and a shed. Pearl showed them a shelf and a small sink attached to the back of the house. She pointed up a well-worn path to the outhouse.

Everyone carried plates from the kitchen to the large table. "Fresh-caught walleye, roasted vegetables, and a lettuce salad with raspberries," Pearl announced. Randall started to eat at soon as his plate touched down and Nika poked him, and gave him a firm glance. He put down his fork until everyone was seated. Nika overcame her nervous stomach and took a bite. The adults asked polite questions about school subjects and Pasadena. After dinner, Pearl took Nika and Randall up the log steps to a long, skinny loft bedroom to settle in for the night. It wasn't completely dark yet, but Pearl said the days would be longer than in California because of how far north they were. She told Nika to try all the bunks until she found the one she liked best, since Randall was just staying the night and this would be her room for the whole visit.

Nika said, "Just like Goldilocks." Pearl had laughed and given her a warm hug. At least she felt comfortable with Pearl. It was different with Ian. Questions tumbled through her mind every time she looked at him, making her speechless and shy. She was glad he'd stayed down in the living room.

The loft bedroom had wooden bunk beds against the inner wall on both sides of the door with only enough room to walk between the bunks and a wall of windows. The bottom bunk of each bed had a big drawer underneath. Extra blankets were piled on one lower bunk. On the far end of the long narrow room was an open closet, with a high shelf and bars for hanging clothes.

Climbing onto the top bunk on the right, Nika could see through the trees to the lake beyond, where the setting sun was coloring the sky. A small shelf with plenty of room for books was sunk into the wall, with a stubby white-barked birch lamp mounted next to it.

"I like this," she said. "It's like a tree house." Randall threw his backpack on the bunk beneath, saying, "You always get the top bunk." She knew he could have chosen the other top bunk if he'd wanted to.

"Help yourself to extra blankets. Nights still get cold at this time of year," said Pearl. "Oh, and Nika." She led Nika to the end closet. "I left some things here you might need." Nika saw a couple of boxes from the drugstore and some plastic wrapped packages. She blushed and nodded.

"Just ask, if you have any questions . . ." Pearl said. Nika was embarrassed but relieved. Pearl would be someone she could talk to, as Meg had been. She smiled at Pearl, then looked over her shoulder. Fortunately Randall was busy unloading his books onto his bunk and not listening.

"You can wash up and brush your teeth using the outside sink beside the porch." Nika remembered on the earlier tour seeing a small sink outside the back door under an overhang. Beside it she'd seen a shelf holding several cups upside down.

After they'd delivered multiple polite "good nights" to Ian and Pearl, it took about three minutes for Randall to climb into bed and fall into a noisy sleep. Nika hauled her backpack up to her new bunk, then stared out the large windows at the semidark, wondering why there weren't any shades. In Pasadena they always had curtains. She didn't like the idea of unknown creatures looking in at her. Nika closed her eyes, wondering what her mom would think, her two children sleeping in the woods under the care of someone she hadn't even sent a Christmas card to for years.

"Nika, wake up. Come on. Would'ya wake up?" Nika dragged her eyes open to see the bouncing blond head of her brother beyond the edge of her bunk.

"What's the hurry?" she answered, her voice slowed by sleep.

"Breakfast!" he shouted. *Leap.* "We made it." *Leap.* "I helped!"

We, she thought. She cast a critical eye at the happiness in charge of his face. So much for Randall having a tough time adjusting.

"In a minute," she said, rolling over.

"No!" he shouted. "Now! We have to go to Big Berry Island so I can go to school with the boys. Hurry!"

Hurrying was not what she had in mind. Sleep was. But she would get up, just for Randall.

"Have some," Randall said, hovering over a plate of steaming pancakes. He looked proudly at Ian.

Nika sat down at the large half-log table and stabbed three. Randall's clothes were covered with flour. For that matter, so were Ian's.

"Where's Pearl?" she asked.

"She had to go to her sister's for a few days," Ian said. "She got a message on the radio early this morning. Her sister fell. She's in the hospital. Pearl left right away and took Zeus."

Did this mean she would be alone in this big house? She'd felt so comfortable with Pearl. She forked a last bite of pancake as Randall thundered out the door. Now it would be just City Kid and New Uncle for a few days.

In the big inboard motorboat, Randall scooted up front next to Ian, pulling on a red and blue life jacket that was too big for him. This left Nika to sit on the bench seat in the back by herself, where she caught the yellow life jacket Ian tossed to her.

As the boat backed and rumbled, Nika thought about

the fact that during this visit, she and Randall would be living apart for the first time ever. Someone else would be watching over him. Someone else would read to him and say good night. She'd expected Randall to be sad and clingy, like he sometimes was, but instead he acted like he'd just won a trip to Disneyland.

Ian gave her a quick glance. "After we come back here and clean up breakfast, you could go with me today. I have a collar I need to check. I told Maki to bring Dramamine," he said. *Great,* thought Nika. Branded by one encounter with a barf bag.

As the boat powered out of the inlet, the reflection of the island broke into pieces in its wake. Ripples of early sun bounced off the water. The air was cool enough, she wished she'd worn something warmer than her light-weight pullover. The life jacket helped, but the wind chilled her arms. Swerving around the shore of the larger island, the wind mixed with cold drops on her face. Waves beat a rhythm on the hull of the boat. She watched the water curl and fold behind them as they picked up speed.

She was trying to picture how these days without Randall would go. What would she do today if she didn't go with Ian? Randall would be in school. She supposed she'd start on the math and science and English make-up work she needed to do. She had to return her homework by June nineteenth, less than six weeks from now. Luckily, she was pretty fast and didn't mind doing it.

They traveled close to the rocky shore of the bigger island. The lake was so large that all she could see was a jagged fence of trees traced against the sky on the far side. She was surprised by how soon the boat careened around the far end of Big Berry Island and slowed. Ian pointed and shouted, "The Camerons' dock!" Randall would be just a short distance away. She could probably even walk across the island to see him.

Three sizes of boys in orange life jackets stood in a line on the L-shaped gray dock, the oldest one a little apart from the younger two. Randall's welcoming party. Ian cut the motor and threw a rope to the oldest boy, who squatted down to pull them in. The smallest boy turned and ran shouting up a path toward several cabins clumped together. Randall remained sitting close to Ian in the boat, then slowly rose to his feet.

Before anyone even said hello, the littlest boy barreled back onto the dock, towing a blond woman by the hand. Then the boy troop descended. The oldest tied the bow rope, and the two youngest grabbed Randall's bags, all at once pulling him from the boat and beginning to lead him away.

The woman had an amused look on her face and called, "Boys! Boys! How about saying hello?"

The boys stopped, bumping into each other as in an old-time movie. They turned to look at their mother and then at Nika, releasing their grip on Randall. The youngest was very blond like his mom.

In a tangle of muttered hellos and shy smiles, they shifted their feet.

"Thank you," she said. "This is Thomas, Gideon, and Jasper." She pointed at each in turn, adding with a smile, "And I'm Claire."

Nika climbed out and stood on the dock, her arms locked in front of her. Ian handed her the stern rope, as if she knew what to do with it.

"I'm Nika, and this is Randall," Nika said, looping the rope loosely on a post, then wrapping and tying it several times to make it secure. The biggest boy was watching her make the knots. He looked about her age. Randall handed his too-large life jacket to Nika.

"Hi, everyone," said Ian from the boat.

"Nika, I'll be right back, okay?" said Randall, and for the first time all morning his face was a landscape of uncertainty. He glanced at the boys, back at her, then back at the boys again.

"Sure, Rand," she said.

Ian jumped to the dock and checked the ropes.

Randall followed the two youngest boys to a small cabin. He came back dressed in an orange life jacket just like the other boys were wearing, carrying his school backpack. Gideon and Jasper clambered into the Camerons' boat and sat on an aluminum bench seat.

Randall came over to Nika. "Gideon's in my grade," he said. His face was serious.

"I'll come see you. We'll do stuff together. You can sleep over," she said. She punched him gently on the arm. When she noticed his new friends watching, she decided to hold back on the sisterly hug.

"Yeah, okay. Later . . ." he said, and punched her back, his smile rebounding. He turned and clambered into the Camerons' boat. Thomas and his mother untied the ropes.

"See you later, Nika," Claire said. "Sorry to be in such a rush. Don't want to be late. Come over for lunch one day. We'll get to know each other." She threw her rope into their boat and climbed down beside Jasper. Thomas lightly hopped into the back, giving Nika a quick smile. Then with one pull he started the motor and backed up before turning to point the bow out into Anchor Lake.

Randall's arm waved a goodbye circle in the air above him as they buzzed away.

The sound of the Camerons' motor faded, leaving an oil smell hanging in the air. Ian busied himself loosening the tangle of ropes she'd made on the post.

He looked as awkward as she felt. They didn't know

a single thing about each other and yet here they were, staring at each other over an undiscovered scrap heap of family history.

"I have a job to do today. We'd better get going." He dangled the rope in his hand. "Ready?"

"I don't think I want to go along," Nika answered.

Ian turned back, his eyebrows raised in surprise. He seemed puzzled. "Well, I could take you into town. I have a friend who works at the library. Or you could stay at Pearl's alone, I guess." He hadn't worked this through.

Nika kind of enjoyed seeing him struggle. "I guess," she muttered.

"This trip might not be one hundred percent fun, but we have to go today," he said almost to himself, looking off at the water.

Then he held out a hand to help her into the boat. "Oh, come on. Come along. You might enjoy it." He looked at his watch. "Could be we'll see a wolf," he added as he started the engine.

As the storm continued to flog the trees, the silvery-tan wolf ran from fence to fence, her legs bent in fear, her ears flattened. With a deafening crack, a huge white pine fell, crushing the fence on one side of the pen. To escape the sounds, the wolf climbed through the branches of the fallen tree, scaled the trunk, and jumped free. She ran cowering through slashing water, through bending and breaking trees. She ran for hours. Finally, exhausted, she slept in shadows. She woke up in a strange forest. Nothing smelled familiar. Slinking behind fallen trees, skirting meadows, she ran again.

Chapter Four

It was weird. It had been so cold earlier. Now the day was almost like Pasadena. Nika dressed in her usual California outfit—ripped skinny jeans, a crop top with a cami underneath, and flip-flops.

Ian took one look and shook his head and pointed to the loft. "You need sturdy long pants, a T-shirt, a long-sleeved shirt, that anorak I had you buy, a hat, and boots. You know the ones from the camping store?" His brow wrinkled. "It's only May. This is unusually warm. It might get cold later."

Nika silently turned and went back up to her room. On the closet floor were the brand-new camping clothes. She tore off the tags and pulled on the khaki pants and a T-shirt. The clothes looked like something from one of Randall's fishing catalogs. She was glad she wasn't going to see anyone she knew.

The stiff new pants whispered as she followed Ian down from Pearl's cabin. Stillness hung like heavy cloth, punctured occasionally by birds that sounded like squeaky wheels and beepers. When Ian and Nika scrambled into Maki's waiting plane, the lake mirrored an upside-down forest on both sides of the inlet.

Maki checked a list and yelled "clear," and they rumbled from the inlet, revving to a roar as the Beaver floatplane plowed the water.

"Got to find the sweet spot for takeoff!" Maki shouted back to Nika as the plane turned in a new direction, then revved up until the pontoons pulled free from the water and the plane lifted into the air.

Nika wasn't as scared this time, and she relaxed against the seat, looking out the window at the trees and lakes below.

"You can listen," Ian said loudly as he adjusted dials on one of the blue metal boxes. He handed the box and headphones to her. "I set it for wolf number three-three-two, from the Stone River Pack." As if Nika could hear anything in this noisy plane! But she followed his gestures and put on the headphones. Radio signals squeaked and crackled and hissed against her ears.

Ian twirled dials on his box and pulled a clipboard

into his lap. He looked back at her and asked, "You take that pill?"

She removed one earphone. "What?" she shouted.

"Did you take the pill?" he yelled back.

Nika nodded. Well, she hadn't, but it was in her pocket, just in case. She hated how Dramamine made her sleepy.

Ian shouted again over the engine noise, "Number three-three-two's signal was in the same place yesterday as it was the day before! Maybe the collar came off!" It seemed to worry him. What worried Nika were the baked-metal smells and the occasional tilting. She took a deep breath and hoped they wouldn't be flying for long.

She looked down at the sea of trees, some of them lime green with new growth. The plane's shadow skittered across the water below. Small islands bristled with trees. How did Maki even know where they were? Everything below looked the same.

Soon they were flying along the edge of a narrow lake shaped like a poorly drawn letter U. On the near shore the forest was slashed through with fingers of black.

Shouting again and leaning back from the front seat, Maki said, "Fire! Last year!" The fewer words the better in a floatplane.

In a little while Nika heard a steady beeping from her blue box. Ian pointed, and Maki eased the plane in that direction. Ian listened, looked down, then waved his hand in a circle. He folded the map into his lap and wrote on a clipboard. Listening, he gestured for Maki to circle a different spot, not too far from the first. Finally he gave Maki a thumbs down.

The plane leaned one wing sharply and circled lower and lower, flying the length of the lake again before coming back to land. Nika held her breath and counted. She knew what he was doing this time—landing into the wind. This time she had no need for a bag. Maki cut the engines thirty feet from a sand beach and drifted until they ran onto the sand with a loud *screech*.

"Horseshoe Lake," Ian said as he climbed out onto the pontoon and then hopped to the sand, beckoning to Nika with a tilt of his head. "Used to be a major logging lake." He leaned his large pack against a rock before coming back to help her.

Maki shouted, "See you at five!" and pulled the cockpit door closed.

Ian tucked his pants into tall, fancy-looking boots and waded back into the water, slowly maneuvering the plane until it was heading out.

"Gotta stay dry this time of year. This water is still really cold," he said as he returned to the beach. The yellow plane lumbered down the lake.

"Why doesn't he stay?" Nika shouted over the noise.

"He also does surveillance for fires. They asked him to do a run today."

Nika watched the plane lift off. When she looked back

at the wall of tightly woven trees and bushes beside the beach, she thought maybe she should have taken that Dramamine and stayed with Maki.

Throwing on his pack, Ian said, "Coming?" He parted some thick branches with his hand.

"Where's the path?" Nika shouted, rooted to the sand.

"We call this bushwhacking," Ian answered as the bushes closed behind him.

Well, she didn't want to be left alone here either. She followed in his wake. As the forest began to wrap around them, she felt a sudden fear. The wind in the tops of the trees whispered and moaned, but where they walked, it felt hot and still. Branches grabbed at her legs and feet. The only sounds were the crunchings and thuds of their footsteps. What if Ian fell and hit his head on a rock? She'd be scuffling for mushrooms and setting snares for bunnies, like people in reality TV shows.

Lots of the trees still had no leaves, just tiny buds and, occasionally, small white flowers. Nika tripped and stubbed her new boots on rocks, tromped through snarls of twigs and fallen logs, grateful that her uncle had made her change, especially the flip-flops. They gradually climbed a small hill where several large trees were snapped off, leaving yellow scars and jagged stumps.

Ian turned his head as he walked and said, "Quite a storm just before you came. Unusual for this time of year. Lots of trees down. It was even worse south and

west of here, where a straight-line wind completely flattened some areas."

They continued up a gradual rise until the trees
thinned and the taller pines took charge. The walking
became easier with fewer bushes to stumble through.
But crisscrossing the forest floor were massive half-rotted
tree trunks so big that she had to sit on them to swing
her legs over.

Ian took a large antenna out of his pack and unfolded
it. It was shaped like three big Ts strapped together. He
plugged the wire into one of the blue boxes. Soon a
rhythmic beeping came from his box. He didn't use the
earphones this time but turned the antenna this way and
that until the beeping got louder. When it did, they hiked
in the direction the antenna pointed.

Every few minutes Ian stopped and listened, pointed,
then walked in a slightly new direction. Nika was hot. So
much for cold in May. She wished now that she hadn't
brought the extra clothes. She took off the anorak and
tied it around her waist. She was down to a T-shirt and a
long-sleeved flannel shirt. Maybe she could just wait right
here. Then she looked at a shadow that seemed to move
beyond the hill and decided, maybe not.

At the top of the rise, she took off her hat. Welcome
soft breezes spread coolness through the damp roots of
her hair. Ian stopped, pulled off his pack, put down the

antenna, and looked at Nika. "I guess I haven't explained much to you about why we do this."

Nika was glad for a break in the walking. "To study them, right?"

Ian nodded. "Wolves live where we can't follow them around very well to see what they're doing. After our hike up here, you can imagine. Anyway, with the radio collars we can track their movements and get an idea of their territories."

"How do you get the collars on?" Nika asked, thinking that she couldn't quite imagine anyone, even Ian, marching up to a wild wolf and sticking a collar on him.

"Well." Ian looked uncomfortable. He took his hat off, ran his hand over his hair, and put his hat back on. "Well, honestly, you've hit upon my least favorite part. Maybe someday we'll invent a better way, but for now we have traps. We pad the trap to avoid injury, but it's still a trap and has to hold the wolf firmly. After catching them, we inject them with a drug to make them sleep. We blindfold them so their eyes won't be damaged. Then we put the collar on and take measurements and blood samples."

"I don't like the trap part," Nika said, wondering how long a wolf might have to wait to be released. She looked to see if Ian minded her speaking up.

"I don't blame you. Most people wouldn't," he said,

"but it allows us to learn things. We need to better understand how wolves and humans can share wilderness areas."

Nika was quiet. Wolves were becoming real to her. There was at least one right nearby. She glanced quickly at the shadowed trees.

Ian settled back on a rock. "Historically, by the mid-seventies, wolf numbers in all of the lower forty-eight states had dwindled to just a few hundred, all located in Minnesota's Superior National Forest. The bounty ended in 1965 and they were declared endangered and protected in 1974. In other places in the world, healthy populations still exist, like Canada, Alaska, and Russia."

He reached over to offer Nika a fruit bar, then continued, "Wolves can live in most of the northern hemisphere as long as they have prey and a chunk of wilderness. And tolerance from humans. Around here their numbers are pretty good since they are protected and studied. Not everyone likes that fact." For a minute Ian seemed to catch himself. "Sorry. I suppose this sounds kind of like a lecture in school."

Nika shrugged. She liked listening to Ian better than stumbling through the woods.

"Why do you like them so much?"

"To me they represent true wildness. They're like we used to be a long time ago living as families, pack members helping to raise the young. Mates can stay together for years. Humans may have learned to hunt large prey as a group from watching wolves. Many people think they have the most complex social behavior of any animal other than primates."

Funny, she thought. He loved the fact that wolves have families, but he spent his time wandering around the world all by himself.

Ian adjusted his heavy pack. "You really got me going! Well, back to work! Ready?" he called over his shoulder, leading the way.

Except for the beeping, they walked in silence now. She could tell by his face that something was bugging him.

The beeping was suddenly louder. Ian held his hand down, his listening posture signaling her not to speak. She dropped beside him as he hunched down behind a grove of scrubby Christmassy trees. Ahead, taller trees provided shade along a ridge of rock.

"We're close," Ian said in a whisper. "The den is through there, in the side of that ridge near an open area. We're pretty sure she had pups this year."

Pups? Prickles of sweat and excitement ran up and down Nika's back and shoulders. She moved a bit closer to Ian.

They waited for a minute or two. Several fat flies dive-bombed Nika's head. Maybe the wolf was watching them.

"The signal should be moving," Ian said in the same

hoarse whisper. He hunched over and moved toward the shade of the large trees, gesturing with his hand that she should stay. No way was she staying by herself with a wolf nearby! She followed, almost stepping on his heels. Off to her right she saw a glint. She tapped Ian's back and pointed. He moved over to the object.

It was a beer can, shiny and new. She was puzzled. What was garbage doing in a remote place like this?

Ian put the can in a plastic bag tied to the side of his pack. He seemed angry. Farther along they found candy wrappers, and another can. Ian stuffed it all into the bag, holding up a hand to remind her to be quiet.

Then abruptly he stood up straight and swore. Apparently they weren't sneaking up on anything anymore. On the ground not far ahead of them was the body of a blackish animal wearing a collar, and it wasn't moving.

Ian reached the wolf first and stood for a long time staring. Nika crowded behind him as he knelt down.

"It's number three-three-two," he said in a quiet voice, "and she's dead. Her stationary signal. I wondered. This part of my job isn't very nice." He took tools from his pack and unbolted a worn collar from the wolf, setting it aside. The collar was heavy leather and canvas, with an attached rectangular box. She guessed the box must be the transmitter that sent out the beeps.

She made herself focus on number 332. The wolf had a rich coat of black with speckles of gray. Her forehead was broad, and her muzzle long. The front feet were bigger than Nika's hand, too big for the graceful long legs. Her body was slightly flattened in death. Her nipples had bare skin around them. Nika reached out to touch the soft fur on her neck. She was so beautiful. She was so big. Nika felt both shocked and confused. If Ian was in charge of studying wolves, why couldn't he prevent this?

"I have to examine her, Nika. I'm pretty sure she was shot, but there's more I need to know. Number three-three-two has been in my study nine years, longer than any other wolf," Ian said sadly, still looking at the motionless body. He placed the pack between his knees and started to unload equipment. "I'm sorry. I probably shouldn't have brought you along." He gave her an apologetic look, then took a leather case from his pack and slammed it on the ground. He stood up and turned around, facing away from her.

Nika figured he was telling her to leave him alone to do his job.

"I'll just sit on that rock over there for a while, okay?" she said. She didn't know what to say to him about the wolf.

"Sure. Fine." Then he added as she walked away, "At least we know for sure she had pups this year."

Nika spun in her tracks, came back, and squatted down. "Where are they?" she asked. If there were pups, they had to do something.

61

"I don't know," he said. "They probably weren't very old. Could be someone killed number three-three-two just to steal them."

"Is that legal?" Outrage filled her voice. She looked off into the woods. Maybe the wolf killer was still out there.

"Actually, no. It's pretty hard to prove, though."

Ian sat back on his heels for a minute. "I really shouldn't have brought you along," he repeated. "I'm really sorry. I'm used to this, but—"

"What about the pups?" she asked again, her eyes searching the forest.

"Most likely they're gone, or dead."

Nika walked away from the dead wolf and Ian. She folded down on the moss of the forest floor and leaned against a huge fallen pine, feeling the comfort of its bulk. She would just hang out within hearing distance and wait.

Nika tried to keep her mind off what Ian was doing. But finally an irrational panic that he might leave caused her to leap to her feet and go to the spot where the wolf had been killed. When she came up behind Ian's bent back, she saw a bloody mess where the beautiful wolf had been. One hand went up to her mouth, and she froze, a grunt of revulsion jammed in her throat.

The wolf was cut open from the chest down to her abdomen, and Ian was examining the exposed area. Dark red blood covered his gloved hands. The bottles beside him were taped and marked, filled with pieces of the wolf. "All of her organs were healthy," he said.

There was no warning this time, and no bag. She threw up, then threw up again, missing Ian's boots by only a few inches.

Ian jumped to his feet, stripped off his bloody gloves, and took her by the shoulders, guiding her to a large rock where he sat her down. He went back to his pack and came back with a can of Pepsi and popped the top.

"Not very cold, no room for ice," he said, holding it out. "A little gross, huh? Obviously, I didn't expect this."

Duh? "Well yeah, but I've seen stuff before," Nika said in a dull voice, looking away, then sneaking a look back again. Yeah, she'd seen a dead squirrel. And a cut-up frog once. She swallowed hard, then swallowed again, and took a drink of lukewarm Pepsi.

She squeezed out the words "What did you find?"

"Two bullets. I'll send them to the lab . . . And now I'm checking to see what she's been eating. I took tissue samples to look for parasites or diseases. Looks like she was facing the shooter," he said. "The ground around her was undisturbed, which means to me that the shooter never touched the body. Just shot her and left."

When he finished the autopsy and cleaned up, he put his tools into the leather case and packed the bottles, stuffing the radio collar into a side pocket. His movements were quick, as though he wanted to get away from this place, something Nika could really understand.

"You're going to bury her, aren't you?" Nika asked. She had begun to shiver.

"What?" he said, then seemed to realize she was serious. "Well. That's a nice idea, but the ground here is mostly rock. It would take a bulldozer to bury her deep enough to keep other animals from digging her up. Scavengers will find her body, and she will return to the earth naturally. Stay here," he said. "I'm going to check something." He walked away in the direction of the clearing.

A hot flush of anger caused Nika to back up, almost tripping. Was he the kind of person to leave what had once been a beautiful animal to rot on the ground? She scraped up armloads of moss and leaves, making several trips to cover as much of the body as she could. At least she'd tried to do something.

Then she kicked at ferns and bushes as she blindly marched back in the general direction they'd come, carrying her Pepsi, her stomach still unsettled. Out of sight of the dead wolf, she stopped and sat down to wait.

But when Ian didn't come, Nika began to feel anxious. She didn't know how long he had been gone. It suddenly felt like a long time. She walked back to the dead wolf's body, stood, and shouted, "Hey, Ian!"

Birds fluttered in dry leaves on the ground. She heard a scraping sound and jumped.

"Ian!" she called, panic rising in her voice.

Then she saw a movement across the clearing. It was Ian, and he was on his knees.

As she moved nearer, he stood up. His face was strangely lit. His clothes were smudged with reddish dirt and bloodstains.

Behind him she could see a tunnel, possibly the wolf's den. Rocks framed the dark entrance. She glanced quickly around for signs of carnage. Nothing.

She looked at Ian again, and his shirt was bulgy.

For a moment his face clouded. "Whoever that stupid jackass was, maybe he left fingerprints on the cans."

The bulge moved.

"Now for the good news. The idiot missed the back corner of the den." He pulled something from his shirt. For a few moments with background music of birdsong and wind, Nika forgot to breathe.

When the silvery-tan wolf tasted new smells and felt new fear, she ran some more. After days of hunger, she tracked the scent of meat. She approached slowly and sniffed. The quick pain of a snare around her foreleg enraged the wolf. She twisted and turned and snapped, then finally collapsed, exhausted. Later, a man lunged at her. She crouched, lifted her lips, and curled onto her back. He jabbed her and covered her head.

Chapter Five

Nika stared at the black-brown sausage of fur with stubby legs cupped in Ian's hands. It had a small wrinkled face, with ears curled down like tiny closed fists.

"The other pups are gone," he said. He turned the pup over, and it squealed and kicked. "It's a male."

She gazed at the pup, amazed by its wildness. It wasn't soft and appealing like dog puppies she had known, with glistening fur and tongue-licked soft ears. She was so lost in the mysteries of the small animal that she hardly heard Ian when he said, "Nika, did you hear me?"

"Sorry, what?" she answered.

"I'm conflicted about this."

"About what?" she answered. The pup was squirming in Ian's hands.

"Well, I should probably let nature take its course."

Nika gave him a fierce look.

"Usually I would. But it isn't a usual situation, the mother being shot." He seemed uncertain. "Also, I suppose the pup is young enough to be socialized for an educational facility. Even if we take him, he still might die. He'll never live wild again."

He had her attention now. The whole world turned a click. Her mouth open, she gaped at Ian.

With sudden urgency he said, "We've got to warm him up. Here. Hold him."

She reached out and gently pulled the pup close, cradling it in her arms, smelling its sharp earthy smell. Its fur was caked with reddish dirt. The soft inner layer of fur was clay colored, the outer layer dark and coarse. Its round belly seemed too big for its body. The small face poked into the folds of her shirt, making little grunts and groans. It was surprisingly strong.

"Okay. You need to carry him against your skin. He's scared. Warmth will calm him," Ian said.

"You mean me?" she asked.

"You heard the 'next to your skin' part, right?" Ian answered.

Nika could no longer make words. She nodded, then nodded again.

Ian raised his eyebrows and said, "Well, let me help you." He instructed her how to tuck the little wolf under her T-shirt and her anorak so the pup could snuggle against her. He tied the sleeves of her flannel shirt like a belt around the bottom of the anorak, to keep the pup from slipping out. "The little pouch will do the trick," he said, surveying their work.

Like a mama kangaroo, Nika thought. Unbelievable. The scratchy warmth and the cold nose bumping her bare belly was one of the best feelings she had ever experienced. As she cradled the shivering bulge with her hands, it quieted.

Nika moved with new purpose now. It was strange how alive she felt with this woolly bundle against her. Something flowed between her and the pup as it swayed with her motion. She fell into the rhythm of Ian's footsteps. Stepping over logs and around rocks, her feet began to feel more agile and certain as they retraced their trail to the beach.

When they reached the beach and were waiting for Maki, Nika asked, "Who would do this?"

"There's a guy from Red Pine who's been known to sell pups illegally. People buy them as pets. He breeds wolves with dogs, too. He once bred foxes for fur, but they all died. It could be him. The authorities shut him down from time to time, but he always gets more animals. He's got problems, hates the government, rants

71

and raves at people on the street." Ian passed a water bottle to Nika. She shifted one hand under the pup, using the other to tip the bottle for a long drink.

"What about the other pups?" she asked.

"I'm sure he wouldn't keep them long. Wouldn't want someone to trace the pups to him. He's been in jail before."

"What about the male? The dad wolf? I thought you said mates stayed together."

"He could have been shot, too. Since he wasn't collared, we'll never know."

Nika glanced down at the lump under her shirt. "How old is he?"

"I'd say less than two weeks. The eyes usually open at about twelve to fourteen days, and his aren't open yet. Which is perfect, really, because we have him before he starts a stage called fear avoidance, something that will happen about the time he opens his eyes. They use their senses, mostly their sense of smell, to recognize the members of their pack. They call it bonding. In humans, it's bonding when a newborn baby attaches to his mom."

They were silent for a moment. Off in the distance they heard the growl of a plane. Ian said, "Let's get ready."

When they were loaded up and pushed out, before Maki started the engines again, Ian said, "Muffle the sound for the pup by holding this jacket over him. He's probably okay since his ears haven't opened yet."

Somehow the pup survived the flight without panic. Ian radioed the vet, Dr. Dave, and arranged for a house call.

Back at Pearl's, when she hatched him out of her shirt bundle, the pup squealed for a few minutes, then became silent again. Nika held him close while Ian set about renovating the screen porch into a pup nursery. "This isn't the first time Pearl's porch has housed a wild orphan," he said.

"Babies are work, no matter how much fun they are," he muttered as he cleared boxes and empty clay pots from the porch. He stuffed a layer of straw into an old wooden box he'd found in the shed. Then he came back with a dog crate with a carrying handle. "We'll let him get used to this, too."

Nika sat on an old sleeping bag on the porch's painted wooden floor. Reality blurred as the pup curled with his nose against her skin. She peeked down through the opening of her shirt. He was just a little loaf, a squirming handful. Ian said he probably weighed only a couple of pounds. When Ian finished the porch, they tried to feed the pup, filling a basting syringe from the kitchen with reconstituted dried milk, but the pup turned his head away and squirmed until he quieted again beneath Nika's shirt.

In Pearl's pile of giveaways in the shed, Ian found a

tattered sheepskin vest. "We can let him cuddle in this. You can't hold him twenty-four-seven. If he was with his mom, he would be down in the den curled up against her most of the time with warm pup bodies all around." Nika put the vest beside her on the sleeping bag for now.

Outside it was late afternoon and beginning to cool down. Ian pulled in another old sleeping bag and secured the plastic on the screens, talking the whole time. "I'm glad Pearl didn't take down this plastic yet. We can do that in a couple of weeks, but for now, it will keep it warmer in here. For such tough animals, wolf pups are pretty fragile at first. I can bring a propane heater from the shed, if we need it."

Nika was lost in another world.

After a few more adjustments to the new porch nursery, Ian left and came back with two ham and cheese sandwiches.

"This will hold us for a while," he said. "I've got to make a trip into town. I'll touch base with Dr. Dave. He's coming out, but I'll need to get supplies, bottles, formula, disinfectant."

Hands on his hips, he paused. "Nika, I feel a little uncomfortable about doing this, but are you okay if I leave you alone for a while?"

"Sure," she said, almost amused. Apparently Ian didn't know how much coping on her own she'd done in the last year and a half. Being left on her own was almost expected. Admittedly, this was a new kind of alone—way out on a wilderness island, alone with a wolf pup.

"Okay," he said, "No sense wasting time. I should be back in less than an hour and a half."

Much later Nika heard two outboard motors, just as the orange light of sunset glowed through the black trees. Ian came through the door and lowered a loaded box onto the porch table. Following him was Dave Hopkins, the vet.

The box overflowed with baby bottles, plastic containers, cans of special formula, and paper towels. Ian hardly spoke, he was concentrating so hard on organizing. After stowing some things in Pearl's gas refrigerator and rattling at the stove, he came back with a plastic nursing bottle of formula that he tested by squirting some onto his wrist, just like on TV.

"We'll hope he takes the bottle. If he doesn't, we can inject some fluids, or think about a feeding tube," Dr. Dave said. "Now let's see the little guy." Nika gently extracted the solid little body from under her shirt. The pup immediately made sharp little whimper sounds and paddled the air with his short legs. Dave lifted him carefully in both hands, laid him on the sheepskin, and gently felt the pup all over. "He's seems pretty healthy. Black pelage, like his mom. And a little powerhouse, to be able to pull himself into a safe corner. The trick will be if he'll eat and how he'll handle the stress."

Nika didn't know what pelage was. Maybe the vet just meant the pup was going to be black. Right now it was hard to say what color he was. Dark earth colored, more than anything.

Ian turned on a goosenecked lamp that hung on the wall. Then he sat down next to Nika and picked up the pup. "I'll give it a go," he said, holding the pup like a baby and brushing the nipple back and forth in front of his nose and lips. The pup let out a squeal, almost a yip, and turned his head away, squirming and twisting in Ian's hands. "Hmm. He doesn't like that too much." He returned the pup to the sheepskin where it nosed in the fur and calmed down.

Nika tried it next, awkwardly holding the bottle toward his bobbing head. Again the pup turned away, pumping his blocky head up and down.

Ian sighed. "We'll try later. He's had a bad, scary time of it. We'll just let him sleep for a bit, then try again."

"If he doesn't take something by midnight," said Dave, "I'll leave the syringe and fluids here for injecting, to keep him hydrated."

Ian stood and put his hand on Nika's shoulder. "Remember, when we first picked this guy up, I said it might not work." He patted her shoulder.

In her head, Nika translated, *The pup could die.* She

turned away. No way, not if she could do anything about it.

Dr. Dave left, and night folded slowly around the island. Wind rattled the plastic on the screens. During the night Ian and Nika tried to feed the tiny pup every couple of hours. But each time he turned his head away. His moans and squeaks seemed weaker. Finally at midnight Ian filled the syringe and injected some fluids under the pup's loose neck skin. A couple of times during the night Ian cleaned the pup's behind with a warm washcloth.

Finally, exhausted, they both settled down in the sleeping bags. Ian placed the pup and the sheepskin vest inside Nika's bag. Ian seemed to sleep, but Nika never did. She lay in the dark and listened to the wind, the rattle of plastic, the groans and squeaks from the pup, and the soft snoring from Ian. Cold filtered through her sleeping bag as the night wore on, and Nika wished she had another blanket.

When the first lances of light pierced the trees, Nika was in a dazed and happy state. The pup needed her. She didn't have time to think about anything else. He was struggling, not wanting to eat. But she knew she could help him. He would eat. He just would.

Ian crawled out of his bag and shuffled around in the kitchen.

Nika got up and went to the outhouse, closing the porch door gently both going and coming back, so it wouldn't startle the pup.

When she sat back down on the sleeping bag, she lifted the pup-filled sheepskin vest. He squeaked and groaned, bumping Nika with his nose.

"Ian!" she called.

Ian answered from the kitchen. "Time to try again? I'll get the formula." He popped quickly into the porch and grabbed a sterilized bottle from the table. In a short time he returned with a nursing bottle full of warmed formula. He handed it to Nika.

"Try it like this. Try squeezing out a little on your fingers, and then put them right under his nose. He might suck your finger. His sense of smell is good even though he doesn't see or hear yet. Then rub the milky nipple by his lips." Nika stared at Ian for a moment. Somehow it was the last thing she ever expected of this wolf-cutting, pack-toting wrinkled-pants science guy, that he would know anything about bottles and babies.

The pup was squirming on her lap, bobbing his heavy little head and squeaking. Nika took the bottle, squeezed some formula onto her fingers, and rubbed it on his lips. His head quivered for a moment, waving back and forth. Gently, she forked one hand under him and touched the nipple to his lips. For a frantic moment he jammed his head around, then grabbed the nipple, sucking so hard at first, he squeezed the nipple shut. Finally as the formula began to flow, he sneezed, and his chubby little paws curled and uncurled. His whole body worked as he sucked down all but a few drops. Finished, the pup slumped down into her lap where he snorted, burped, and fell asleep. Neither Nika nor Ian said anything for several minutes. Nor did they move. They smiled at each other in silence.

"That's more like it," Ian finally said.

Switching to teacher mode, he said, "Next essential. Maybe you noticed me doing this last night, but now that he's eating, bathroom chores become more important. I'll show you what to do." *Olivia would never believe this,* Nika thought, as Ian set the sleepy pup on a diaper pad. He had brought a bowl of partially heated water and a piece of torn-up old towel. "We want to make sure everything is used once and washed." He paused. "Remind me to introduce you to Big Bertha later on, Pearl's ancient wringer washer that she keeps in the shed. Even though we live with outhouses, we have a well and a generator for electricity. Propane heats the water. A bit time-consuming, but it works. Nature does the drying."

He proceeded to dip the towel and to wipe the pup's bottom. Then he took fresh towel bits and wiped again, picking up messy parts with paper towels. "Just like mom's tongue," he said. Nika covered her mouth so Ian wouldn't see the face she couldn't help making.

"Anyway," Ian said, putting the clean pup back in the vest, "pups are very vulnerable to disease at this age. In the wild, cleaning keeps the den fresh, making fewer smells to attract predators." He removed the pad. "You'll get used to it."

He stood. "I'll make us some breakfast. We've got to eat, too." Suddenly Nika realized she was starving. Since waking this morning in the porch with the pup next to her, all she'd thought was *What if he doesn't eat? He's got to eat. What if he doesn't?*

But he did. Four whole ounces!

Their day became a team effort of mixing formula, feeding, cleaning the pup's bottom, cuddling, napping, reading, mixing, feeding, cleaning, cuddling, and napping, operating Big Bertha, and hanging out laundry. Weighing with a sling scale was added to pup duties. Officially, the pup weighed in at two pounds, two ounces, his first day. Ian estimated his age now at about ten or eleven days. He made a chart to keep track of dates, eating, and weights that hung on a clipboard by the kitchen door. A routine was established. Nika had little time to think about much else.

"Shall we both sleep out here again tonight?" asked Ian that afternoon. "Don't worry about it, if you're too tired. I don't think you slept much last night. And it gets cold."

"You snore," she said, rolling her eyes.

"If you want some real sleep, I think I could handle this guy by myself. Then we'll set up a schedule. Maki said he would help a few nights or days. A new research assistant is coming soon. I'm sure she'd be delighted. Dr. Dave has a volunteer. And Pearl, of course, when she comes back. Even Zeus will help. We'll have a whole pup team!"

Nika thought for a moment. Why all those people? In a way, she liked it with just the two of them. Nika was already beginning to feel like this black furry milk guzzler was really hers.

"He's so tiny. You and I can take care of him ourselves, don't you think?"

Ian smiled.

"I'll stay," Nika answered firmly, not looking at Ian. "I'll sleep here. But I'll need another blanket." She kept her eyes on the pup. "Maybe tonight he'll sleep better and not squirm around so much."

Ian picked up a briefcase and took out some paperwork. "Never fear—he'll wake us up."

Nika looked to see if he was amused by this idea. It was the kind of thing people laughed about together. But she couldn't tell.

Later they both settled in for the night, reading by headlamps as the pup nestled in the sheepskin inside Nika's unzipped sleeping bag. The extra blanket was beside her. As he clicked off his headlamp, Ian said, "We're going to have to pup-proof this porch pretty soon. He's going to be all over it, chewing anything that's loose. Anything with a cord, for example. And we'll need a baby gate for the door."

They were silent for a minute. Then Ian's voice came through the dark, more serious now.

"You know, Nika, a wolf pup is not a pet, not a dog. However much we get him to accept us, he's still a wild animal, with the needs of a wild animal."

"I know," Nika said, her voice low. Of course she knew the pup was a wild animal. Of all people, she knew not to get her heart set on anything.

In the dark, as she listened to the pup's wheezing snores and moans, she reached out her hand to feel the rise and fall of his breathing. She snuggled down. Just touching him, she felt better.

The silvery-tan wolf patrolled the small pen with cautious steps. The smells of other animals wafted through the air. When the man threw scraps of meat over the fence, his mouth twisted to the side. The wolf hunched and froze behind a pile of lumber. In her corner she began to dig. Each day she dug with new energy. Her large paws became dark with dirt. And in the night, the rich dark smells of earth called her to dig some more. When she slept, her paws moved in her dreams.

Chapter Six

For a minute Nika couldn't remember where she was. The moon floated through the tall trees beyond the porch. Moonlight smudged the cloudy plastic sheets fastened over the screen walls. The gooseneckd lamp shed a small apron of light. Then she heard tiny moans and groans coming from the sheepskin vest beside her. Short fat legs propelled the small sausage shape a few inches closer to Nika's side, a cold nose bumping her hand in the semidark. The pup was awake. And probably hungry. She scooped the tiny round-bellied body close to her.

"Ian," she called. A second lamp clicked on, and Ian pulled himself out of his sleeping bag.

"Told you," he said. He sounded tired. Ian walked barefoot into the kitchen, where he clattered around. In a few moments he came back with a bottle. "We'll try a little more than four ounces this time." He handed it to her, pulled over a cushion, and sat down on the floor next to her.

Holding the pup as she had before, sitting cross-legged, one hand under his chest, she placed him so his front paws could push against her knee. When she put the bottle next to his mouth, the pup's head wobbled and bumped, knocking the nipple away. His legs flew, pushing himself almost off her lap. She lifted him back and held him in the crook of her arm, offering the milky nipple again by rubbing it over his lips. He quivered, grabbed hold, then drank quickly, noisily pulling, jerking and nosing the bottle, his paws opening and closing. His eyes were still tightly closed.

"When he wants to eat, he doesn't fool around, even when he can't see!" she said, smiling.

After the pup finished, they cleaned his bottom with the washcloth. His moans subsided to tiny short groans, and Nika placed him back in the sheepskin. Ian returned to his bag and clicked out the lamp.

As she stretched out, Nika noticed that her sleeping bag smelled slightly of wood smoke. Maybe from a long-ago campfire. In the distance she heard the low muttering of thunder. Before she fell asleep, she ran some mental movies of Pasadena, thinking of the bottlebrush tree in front of Meg's house. It seemed impossible that just a week ago she had touched the electric red blossoms. How could two places be so different? She imagined telling her mom about the moaning, snuffling wolf pup roughly breathing at her side. It had been more than a year and a half since she'd lost her mom, but Nika could still hear her laugh.

In the morning the new leaves glistened from the night rain. Dave came early to check the pup. With him was a volunteer from his office named Lorna. Dave showed them all how to sterilize shoes by stepping into a bleach solution in a dishpan outside the door. He explained it was to prevent the pup from contracting dog diseases while he was tiny and vulnerable. He also brought a baby gate for blocking the doorway into the house. Not that they needed it yet.

Lorna crouched too close to the pup's face, cooing and talking baby talk in a high voice. Immediately, Nika disliked her.

"Hi," Nika said, forcing a smile. Lorna was probably in her late twenties with streaked blond hair messily clipped on top of her head.

The girl didn't even look at Nika. "Can I hold him?" Lorna asked, smiling at Ian, reaching for the pup.

Nika looked helplessly at her uncle. A volcano of

protectiveness welled up from her very center and was threatening to erupt.

Ian stepped in. "For a week or so, we are going to just have Nika, Dave, and me holding and feeding the pup. After his eyes are fully open, and he's getting around, I'm sure we'll be grateful for some extra help."

"Okay, but here." Lorna pulled a large stuffed-bear pillow from a shopping bag she'd carried into the porch. "Someone gave it to my brother. I thought the wolf might play with it."

Nika reached for the bear and said, "Nice." It seemed ten times the size of the tiny pup. What was Lorna thinking?

But Ian raised his eyebrows. "That bear will come in handy. It's furry. It might offer him some comfort. Thanks, Lorna."

Lorna gazed at Ian, carefully arranging herself against the wall. "So, Nika, what grade are you in?" she asked, glancing at Nika before beginning a careful inspection of her polished nails.

"Oh, that varies from year to year," Nika answered, politely smiling but suddenly getting up and heading for the kitchen.

She felt better after Dr. Dave and Lorna left. But after a few hours passed and it came to be time for another feeding, Lorna was still on Nika's mind.

"Don't you think it's better for the pup not to have much company when he's so small?" she asked when they were getting the bottle ready. "I mean, like what Dr. Dave said about dog diseases and everything,"

"Well, of course, we need Dave to do checkups. But yeah, I agree."

"Dave's nice," she said as she got down on the floor in a cross-legged position and picked up the squealing pup. As she was feeding him, she noticed something wrong with his right eye, like a little hole in the lid. "Ian!"

When he came to inspect, he laughed. "What do you think's happening?"

She looked again more carefully. The pup's right eye was slowly opening, like a tiny zipper, starting from the inside corner. A couple of hours later when she picked him up again, the pup looked at Nika through one milky blue eye. Ian said that the pup's eyesight was quite fuzzy and he couldn't hear yet, but still, seeing her, seeing them, smelling them, he would remember. After a cleaning the pup sat on her lap with one eye open, and she let him suck on her finger. Needle-sharp baby teeth were growing in too—his upper canines and incisors, Ian said. By the next feeding the left eye had started opening as well. Nika gently washed both eyes with a clean cloth. The left one still stayed half shut. The pup wasn't exactly cute. He was stubby, rough like unwashed wool, with button-down ears. But in her mind he was beautiful.

o o o

After the next feeding, Ian said, "This might be a good time to go see Randall for a while. Tell him and the boys about the pup. It will give you a little break."

"He'll want to come see."

"They all will. But not yet. I'll stay with the pup. Try to think of a name while you're walking. Go on, take a hike," he insisted, laughing. "When you come back, I have some stuff to show you. Ms. Fish sent a few more materials from your school, to complete this year's credits. Also, I had an idea. You could do a project about the pup—do some reading and write a log with notes about his development. How many kids would have something like that to turn in?"

Nika went to the outdoor basin to wash, then up to the loft for some fresh clothes. When she followed the path Ian had showed her down past his cabin and across the sand spit up onto the Big Island, all she could think about was the pup. She didn't like leaving him. Maybe his other eye would open completely and he would look at Ian and like Ian better by the time she came back. That was stupid, she knew, especially since Ian had said the pup wouldn't see very well. But she remembered what she'd learned about how important those first days were, the days when a pup bonded with his pack.

On the other side of the sand spit, Nika followed the trail up a rocky hill. The air was spring cool, the sun hidden in a dishwater sky. As she entered the tall trees, the forest surrounded her like an army. A few days ago the smells of damp earth and pine needles in the sun had been new to her. Today she felt like she knew this place. Low branches touched her face. A jungle-sounding bird squawked, drumming rhythms far off in the trees. The hushed buzz of tiny leaf life enlivened her senses, and she was alert to every sound.

In a little more than fifteen minutes of walking, she saw green roofs through the trees. She hoped Randall hadn't been too sad without her. The six months after Mom had died, before they were finally sent to Meg's, had been a time of endless waiting. For people to pick them up to give them rides. For social workers. For adults to make decisions. During that time Randall would never go to sleep unless she sat beside his bed. At school, too, she had stood up for him. Now she could hardly wait to tell him about the pup.

The boys' bunkhouse shook with shouts and pounding. It sounded like a whole troop of boys, not just four. She knocked, and Randall exploded out of the door. Two small boys streaked around him.

"Neeks!" he shouted. "There was a bear last night, trying to get the bird food! Thomas's dad said it'll probably come back. Tonight we're going to watch with our flashlights!"

Nika hugged Randall's skinny body. "Really, Randall?" Her little brother seemed so sure of himself, so caught up in his new life with these strangers.

He pulled away. "You don't believe me? Just ask Thomas!" Then he ran back into the bunkhouse, letting the wooden screen door smack shut behind him. Nika followed him in.

Standing on one side of the room were three sets of bunk beds, and on the other a couple of old stuffed chairs faced a shiny green metal wood stove. Boy stuff littered the floor: clothes, flashlights and shoes, comics, pop cans, and not-so-clean plates. A smell of wet socks hung in the air. There was a whole city of action figures and cards and some colorful books in the center of the floor. Over by the door was a heap of wet swimsuits, towels, socks, and life jackets. Fishing poles leaned against the wall by the door. Randall heaven.

"Okay, Thomas, what about this bear?" Nika asked of the oldest boy, who was on one of the top bunks reading.

Thomas looked at her with certainty in his steady gaze. She wondered if he was in her grade. He seemed comfortable in his role of being the oldest.

"Yeah, there was," he said, then returned to his book as if it were no big deal. "Once in a while one comes around . . ." He cut another glance at Nika, perhaps wondering whether she would react in some shrieking-girl way.

"See!" Randall said, practically shouting.

"So Randall, besides that, how are you?" she asked, pulling out the Twins cap he'd left in Pearl's loft and handing it to him.

"Great! Wow, my hat!" Randall took the hat from her and put it on his bunk. He was not exactly in a talkative mood. Nika settled into the chair. Randall kept looking at Nika as if he didn't quite know what to do with her in his new world.

After a while the two younger boys ran back into the cabin and started sorting out their stuff. "Mom says clean up before we go," one of them said. In a flurry they jammed game pieces onto shelves next to the wood stove.

Then they grabbed their suits and towels and raced back out, shouting, "Lunch is ready, and then we can go out in the boat after—"

"Yeah, okay!" Randall shouted back, hurrying to gather what was left from the floor.

"Randall," Nika said slowly, "did anyone tell you about the wolf pup?"

"Yeah, Claire did. Can we see it?"

"Not quite yet. When he settles in a bit and he's more used to people. So you're okay then?"

"Well, yeah," he said, as if she should know. "Want to go fishing?"

"No. I gotta get back to the pup."

"That's okay," he answered brightly, almost seeming relieved.

After how much he'd once needed her, it pinched a little to see him so happy without her.

"Let's go eat." Nika jumped up from the chair and wrestled with Randall, enjoying for a minute the once-familiar closeness of her brother. His wiry strength surprised her as he broke free, shouted for his friends, and ran from the cabin.

One morning the man staggered toward the pen barking out harsh words. He had a metal stick in his hands and waved it around. The wolf hid in her corner, then clawed her way deeper into the hole she'd dug, frantic and afraid. Her strong paws flew. Suddenly, air rushed into the tunnel. She slipped her body through, out into the sweet sharp smells of freedom.

As the silvery-tan wolf left the road and felt the forest ground beneath her feet, something tore through the leaves, followed by a boom. She ran faster.

Chapter Seven

Claire Cameron was like one of those moms from Nika's old school, neatly dressed in clean jeans and a trim plaid shirt, blond hair cut in a short bob, confident in the way she moved and smiled.

"Welcome, Nika. How was the walk over?" she asked, putting a plate of turkey and cheese sandwiches on the table with a large glass pitcher of juice. Everyone plopped into chairs and began speed-eating. Claire Cameron could probably feed four boys in her sleep.

"Okay," Nika answered.

"Are you going out in the boat with Jake and the boys?"

"No, I'll just head back. Say, is there a path along the shore?"

"Yes, there is," Claire answered. "It's practically a highway of smooth rock. There's even a small beach along the way, probably the best swimming spot on the island." Bringing over a bowl of grapes and apples, Claire studied Nika for a minute.

"I heard about the pup. That will keep you busy!" She laughed. "What will happen with the pup in the fall, do you know? Does Ian have some sort of plan?"

Nika looked at Claire and shrugged. But inside she felt a crash. Of course Ian would have ideas about the pup's future. Right now she didn't want to ask. First, she needed a plan of her own. Maybe she could take the pup back to Pasadena with her. He would still be small then, wouldn't he? Olivia's mom was always rescuing animals. Nika was glad when Claire dropped the subject.

After they finished eating, Thomas said, "Dad said meet him at the dock," and the boys rushed out as if it were a rule that boys in a group must run. Clearing her own things to the sink Nika said, "Well, thanks for lunch," not wanting to stick around for any conversations about the pup's future.

Standing on the cabin steps, Nika watched as Randall and Thomas put their things together on the dock. It was good that he was so happy. Just like Meg used to say: We need to learn to depend on other people, not just on each other.

Nika shouted at Randall, "Have fun!" and called back through the door to Claire, "Thanks again!" The boys were already in the boat. The father had loaded poles and gear.

"'Bye, Neeks!" yelled Randall at the tops of his lungs.

After finding the path by the water, Nika began to walk along the smooth shoulders of the rock formations. Looking ahead, she saw giant boulders perched there as though they had been thrown by a giant's hand. She wondered about the bear the boys had talked about and felt uneasy.

The sky began to clear when Nika was nearly halfway across the Big Island, going along the shore. Just as she was beginning to relax, she heard a crash in the woods. A large blackish animal with no tail raced away. It was kind of chubby and ran with a rocking motion. In an instant, she knew. She froze. But it was racing away from *her*, as though she were some Tyrannosaurus rex in jeans and a sweatshirt! After some minutes of taking deep breaths to control her fear, she continued on. The bear seemed to be headed toward the center of the island. She didn't know much about bears, but there were plenty of scary stories about them, enough to keep her hyperalert, watching for shadows in the trees. Her comfort in this new place was shaken.

One way to avoid watching for bears every minute was to distract herself by thinking of a name for the pup. She thought of her favorite photograph of a wolf, one she had cut out of a magazine at home and put in a scrapbook. The wolf looked regal, his chin held high; he looked proud, strong. Princely. But Prince was too corny. A dog's name. A royal name would be good, though. She remembered last year in English class when they read a legend about Shan Yu, the Blue Wolf of Mongolia, and how the great Genghis Khan was called the Blue Wolf.

"Khan," she said, stopping for a minute to speak out loud to the rocks and trees and lapping water. "I'm going to call him Khan."

Aiming for the flattest rocks, she began to hop along again, excited to tell Ian about the name. Ahead a smooth rock jutted out, like a giant's arm resting in the water. There were footholds in the steep side, and she soon found herself surrounded on three sides by water, high and dry and far from trees. There was one boulder on the top of this rock shelf, as though dropped there by someone. It might make a nice backrest. She plopped down, leaned, and watched Randall's boat disappear behind an island on the far side of the lake. She felt the sun on her skin. The rock reassured her. There were no more crashing sounds. Confidence trickled back into her body.

Down from her rock and just ahead a small yellow band of beach nestled in a cove. It looked private and protected. This must be the Big Berry swimming beach Claire had talked about. Maybe she'd go there and get her feet wet.

When she looked out at the large lake again, three clouds hung in the bright blue sky, as if they'd been stuck up there with tape. In the distance a couple of fishing boats were dots on the water. She lay back, feeling the sun's warmth seep up from the rock into her body. The sloshing sounds of the water made her sleepy.

Nika awakened to the sound of a hollow metal banging, as when oars hit the sides of an aluminum boat. A motor coughed and died. She heard a man's voice swearing. Ugly knifelike words. Words she didn't expect to hear lying on this rock, but words she'd heard before. She sat up to see a man standing unsteadily in the back of a fishing boat. He seemed to be about to land at the small beach. His words slurred, he shouted something like "Good for nothing animal, I'll kill her when I find her . . ." The man had a long untrimmed beard and shapeless tan clothes. He held on to a pole. Suddenly he spotted her, lost his footing, and sat down hard on the aluminum seat. For a minute he just stared.

Nika stood up and yelled, "Get out of here!" In moments her feet moved so fast she was hardly aware of sprinting across the broad surface of the rock and bounding into the woods. She kept running until she was out of breath. When she stopped to listen, she heard a motor start up. She continued breaking through the woods until she found the center path, looked quickly for bears, then jogged the rest of the way back to the sand spit that linked the two islands.

When Nika reached the crossing, she hid behind some bushes, looked down the inlet, and listened. There was no one. She ran across. The bear had been a little scary, but nothing like that creepy man. Why had he been poking around? What animal was he yelling about?

Back at Pearl's, she sterilized her shoes and entered the screened and plastic-enclosed porch. Ian was half asleep on his sleeping bag, a large pile of books beside him. The pup was on Ian's chest, wobbling on its stubby legs.

"Your turn," he said, getting up and placing the pup on his bag, where it teetered and fell over. Ian directed her to the kitchen, and to the written instructions for making formula, now typed and posted on the cupboard door.

She concentrated on getting the formula proportions right and warming it to the perfect temperature. With the bottle in her hand, she stepped over the baby gate into the house.

"Ian," she said, "I saw this guy with a long beard in a boat by Big Berry Beach. He didn't land or do anything, but he swore a lot, saying he was going to shoot some blankety-blank animal. Then he drove his boat away." She handed him the bottle.

Ian sat feeding the pup with his shoulders pulled forward, a worried expression tightening his eyes. "Did he speak to you or threaten you?" His voice was tense. The pup pulled away from the bottle, and Ian calmed him.

"Nooo," she said, letting the word stretch and linger. She shrugged. "I thought he was just some drunk."

"What did he look like? Did he have a gun?"

She had to think. Uncertainty kept her from giving a good description. All she could remember was the long pole. "No, I don't think so."

"You know he's gone?" Ian asked, pacing toward the door, then back again.

"I think so, but I couldn't tell. I was running. He started his motor."

Ian paused and seemed to be thinking. "When you go over to the Big Island, find someone to go with you," he said firmly.

"Okay." His brisk manner startled her, as if maybe she had done something wrong.

Later, as they sat eating their supper of cold chicken and asparagus and leftover muffins, Nika said, "I thought of a name for the pup."

"Tell me." Ian passed her the honey.

"Khan," she said. "You know, K-H-A-N, like a prince."

When Ian didn't say anything right away, she asked, "Do you like the name?"

"Perfect," he said. He seemed to be thinking about something else. "A prince . . ."

She told him then the story of the Blue Wolf and what they'd read in school.

"Well, I hope he isn't going to be like Genghis Khan, rampaging around destroying things," said Ian. "Maybe our Khan will just conquer hearts." She looked at him to see if he had really said what he said. Our Khan.

She had to admit, it was a cool thing to say.

That night she prepared formula for the last feeding before going to bed. After she came back to the porch and sat down, Ian handed her the pup. She settled the frantic little bundle between her left arm and her body and rubbed the nipple on his lips. There was energy in his grab, and he sputtered as he squeezed too hard again. She gently inserted her finger into the corner of his mouth to release the hold and started again. This time he drank it down in steady gulps.

"Well done, both of you," said Ian, staring with admiration at the pup, who looked at them with two open milky blue eyes. Before long Khan's eyelids slumped, and he curled into the sheepskin, where he fell into a milk-induced sleep.

"Maybe we'll sleep tonight," said Nika. Ian laughed and gently touched her on the head as he stood up and crossed the room.

The tan wolf hid in the shadows of the forest. Before many days passed, hunger drew her back toward the pens. Hearing angry shouts again, she ran. The sounds of snapping and booms fell behind her. This time she angled up a rocky hill following the smell of water. As she came out of wind-fallen trees, she saw the ground fall away to a lake below. She scrambled down, leaped into the water, and swam toward a nearby island. Overhead an eagle circled, screeching. Its shadow slipped across the body of the fleeing wolf.

Chapter Eight

What was that high-pitched wail? Nika briefly opened her eyes in the dark, then closed them. Curling away from the sound, she pulled deeper into her bag. She just wanted to go back to sleep. She was sliding back into a dream.

> There was no sound in Nika's dream. She and her mom and Randall were sitting on the ground beside a waterfall in smog-filled southern California heat. Her mom smiled, her mouth moving with lost words. Her long wheat-colored hair coiled over her shoulder. Nika looked at the aqua blue pool beneath the falls. All three of them stood and pulled

off their T-shirts. Nika's new bathing suit was bright red. Randall's blue shorts looked three sizes too big on his small bony body. Nika ran to be the first one in. The cold water sparked across her hot skin. She smiled as she rolled in the comforting arms of the water. Then through the underwater blue she saw her mom swim away, her outline lost in a blur of water. In just a second of time, her mom was gone. Nika kept swimming, trying to follow, wanting to shout out, but she couldn't. Then a strange high-pitched sound traveled through the water, and she pulled to the surface and gasped.

"Nika?" said a low rumbling voice.

Where was she? Why didn't her mom come to wake her? What was that sound? She was so tired.

"Nika, are you okay? Nika, did you hear the pup howl?"

Again, out of the darkness came a thin high-pitched sound. Suddenly she knew where she was and sat up. Ian clicked a switch, making an island of light in the corner of the porch. Out in the middle of the floor, all by himself in a pile of straw, was Khan, his head tipped up, sitting, his little front legs bracing him. He let out another miniature howl that turned into a whine at the end. She stood up and walked over, plopping down near him. She could feel the cold floor through her sweatpants. When Khan discovered she was there, he staggered up to her with bouncy steps.

"Look, he's trying to run," she said to Ian, who had returned to his bag. She wasn't the only one who was completely worn out.

"He howled off and on for about five minutes, but I guess you didn't notice," mumbled Ian from his bag. "You'll have to put that in your log. First howl at twenty days old."

The pup snuffled up into her lap. "And," she answered, "he's hungry."

"I'll do the honors." Ian slowly unfolded from his bag and stretched before going into the kitchen.

So many changes had happened since the pup's eyes opened. It was hard to believe it was already May twentieth. Feeding Khan every two hours, and dozing on the floor, had worn out both Ian and Nika. Pearl was due home in a couple of days, and Nika was looking forward to her help with Khan. While the pup slept, she'd been plowing through Ian's stack of books on wolves for her science report, making notes on cards. She couldn't believe how many he had on the subject. She wrote new notes every day, such as "Pups are in the neonatal stage from birth to when eyes open." And "Wolf pups use all of their senses to identify and bond with their caregiver."

Khan could already tell her apart from someone else, just using his sense of smell.

Today after she finished logging pup behavior, Ian called from the kitchen, "Breakfast!"

As they ate, he laid out the day. "Lorna is coming to pup-sit today. I have errands in town, and thought we would take the boys with us. You can spend some time with Randall, get to know the town a little, and take a break. Pup care is pretty demanding."

"Not Lorna," Nika said. "I don't mind, really. We can leave him once Pearl comes back."

Ian shot her a look. "Yeah, I know, but Lorna is eager to help, and Dave would like her to have the experience. We can show her the routine before we go."

Nika stabbed her fork into the yolk of the over-easy egg and watched it spill onto the white. What could she say? Ian had this thing about needing a team. "Why do I need to get to know the town?" she asked.

He just looked at her and delivered a slice of buttered toast. "Lorna should be here by ten." He cleared his plate. "Your turn to wash the dishes."

For a minute she contemplated returning to her bag for a few more minutes of sleep, but then she'd just have to wake up again. She clunked the dishes and pans around loudly in the hot soapy water.

By the time she was finished, Nika could hear Lorna's

loud chirpy voice as she was crossing the rock ledge. Then the front door thumped shut, and she heard voices talking, and footfalls in the living room.

"Hiieee," Lorna said. Nika nodded from where she slumped, her elbows on the kitchen counter.

As Lorna and Ian approached the door to the porch, Nika glanced over her shoulder and called, "You gotta do your shoes!"

"Oh, that's right. I almost forgot. Thanks for reminding me, Nika," Lorna said, smiling with her perfect white teeth. She stepped quickly to dip her shoes into the bleach solution at the porch door, grinning at Ian the whole time. Was Lorna trying to impress Ian? Nika wondered. After all, he was single. And not bad looking for forty-two.

Lorna listened open-mouthed to Ian's instructions about how to handle the pup. Not that she paid attention. She bent down and leaned into the wooden box to grab the pup.

Wouldn't do that, Nika thought, but didn't say anything. The pup squealed and growled and snapped, jamming his short legs into reverse.

Ian looked at Nika, who rolled her eyes upward.

Using a patient teacherly tone, Ian said, "So, Lorna, like I said, maybe it's best if you let him come to you. Just sit for a while and when he comes out, find something to attract him. He likes a pine branch or dog toys like the

113

stuffed lobster. Don't play tug or let him bite on you. He should be hungry in a couple of hours. There's formula in the fridge. Warm it in hot water in a pan—just like you would for a baby. Lay him on the stuffed bear to feed him the first time since it's familiar and it's furry. You'll be fine. He'll sleep most of the time."

"I'll stay, too," said Nika quietly, appealing to Ian with narrowed eyes.

"Nope, you're coming with me," he answered, his tone of voice like a closing door.

They picked up Thomas and Randall at the Camerons' dock and sped off across Anchor Lake. Randall sat up front next to Ian on one of the large cushioned seats. An awning covered the front part of the boat. Randall had his eyes on Ian and was grinning. It was sunny and windy and cool, and Nika was glad she remembered her anorak this time. It was still May, and while many days had been almost like summer, she had learned the weather could change fast. She tucked her arms inside her life jacket and looked over at Thomas beside her in the stern. When the boat had first picked up speed, their faces got wet from spray. They both laughed and ducked down. The lake ahead opened into a beautiful silver expanse, chiseled by waves. The boat bounced and thumped the waves. When Nika glanced over at Thomas again, he pulled down his wet baseball cap and grinned, showing a mouthful of braces.

When they were partway into town, Ian called loudly over the sound of the engine and the splashing waves, "I'm going to buzz by that eagle's nest I told you about!"

They arrived at the back side of a small island, across a narrow passage of water from the town of Red Pine. Ian cut the engine and pointed up. The eagle's nest was at the top a giant white pine. It was as big as a queen-size bed, made of sticks woven together and balanced on three heavy top branches.

"This year two chicks hatched," he said.

He handed the binoculars back to Nika. Randall slipped in back to sit beside her, eager for his turn to look. Nika could see something brownish moving, maybe a head, just over the edge of the nest. She handed the binoculars to Thomas.

"Looks like a chick, maybe," Thomas said, as the boat idled in a low rumble, rocking with the waves. It was hard to keep the binoculars steady.

"Guys, look quick! One of the adults!" Ian pointed to a white pine to the right of the nest tree. The bird lifted high into the air, dipped its pure white head, then shot downward, hitting the water with its talons extended. As the eagle pulled from the lake, shedding a curtain of water, a fish more than half the length of its body hung from its grasp. With long swoops of its powerful wings, the bird carried its prize to the nest.

"Dinner for the kids," Ian said. Two small scruffy heads poked up from the nest.

"Who's feeding them? Is it the mom or the dad?" Nika asked.

"They both feed the chicks. It could be either one."

As they rounded the end of the island, heading toward the town docks, Nika thought about how amazing it was that a dad eagle actually brought food to his chicks. She never knew that before.

Since Thomas lived in Red Pine during the school year, he knew every inch of town and seemed excited to show Randall and Nika around. The three of them set off to find hot dogs and ice cream, agreeing to meet Ian back in front of the hardware store at three-thirty.

They ate lunch in the park next to the ice cream place. Two gray jays perched on the bench beside them, cocking their heads and politely accepting bits of food.

Thomas leaned toward Randall and Nika and said, "You two want to go see the crazy man of Red Pine?"

Nika's mom had taught them never to make fun of people who were different. She and Randall just looked at each other, then back at Thomas without saying anything.

"Yeah, well," Thomas said, sensing their hesitation, "actually, we wouldn't really talk to him or do anything mean, but he's got lots of wild animals in cages. The authorities are always trying to find a way to take his animals away. I guess he used to run a game farm back in the dark ages."

Nika remembered what Ian had said about the man who captured wolf pups to sell, who once had foxes. Could this be the man who had taken Khan's siblings, who had killed Khan's mother? "Let's go," she said, feeling a blaze of anger.

Thomas stood up, and they started to walk, dumping their garbage in a nearby can. "My dad says this guy likes animals better than people. Except his cages are too small and he starves them when he can't feed them."

"What's his name?" Nika asked as they followed Thomas out of the park.

"Bristo. I never heard him called anything else. Just Bristo. He has a potbelly, and a long beard, and he yells at kids."

Nika remembered the man in the boat off Big Berry Island. She felt a chill.

"What animals does he have?" asked Randall.

"Some funny-colored foxes, I think. Then the wolf he just got, a big dog, some skunks that don't stink, raccoons, and a mountain lion. I heard sometimes he sells wolf puppies to people for pets. My dad say it's not only illegal but they make bad pets. He says people hardly ever keep them once they're grown."

Thomas led them up the main street, turning after several blocks onto an unpaved street where the houses got more and more dilapidated as they walked.

Finally they approached a decaying wooden fence that ran along the street, then cut back to connect with a shack made of unfinished gray boards. It was in the last row of houses. Tall trees hung over the bare lot beside the shack. Old machine parts lay about, sunken in tangled grasses. Hand written No Trespassing signs were posted on the wooden fence next to other signs with misspelled words about the government and freedom and taxes. Apparently the same freedom didn't apply to the animals he kept. Through missing slats in the fence, Nika could see pens made with rusty wire or chain link. A strange cough-scream from one of the pens caused them to stop so fast, Nika almost fell.

In a quiet voice Thomas said, "It's better to walk right up to the cages in the open, rather than sneaking. I've heard stories of buckshot tearing through the leaves over kids' heads when they spied from the bushes." With Thomas going first, they went around the end of the rickety fence, past the shed, and walked slowly across the bare yard.

They didn't see anyone, so they kept going toward

the pens. The first pen was the size of a small bedroom. A crooked wooden lean-to huddled in one corner under the shade of a scrubby pine. On the roof of the lean-to was a cougar. He must have made the cough-scream noise they'd heard. Nika let herself breathe again when she saw the heavy wire fencing that went over the top of his cage as well as along the sides.

They stood away from the wire and watched the cougar's tail make question marks in the air. After a while the tail relaxed and just twitched at the tip. The animal never moved. His sand-colored eyes looked straight past them, through them. He was skinny and worn like an old fur coat.

"Kinda creepy," said Randall. "He just stares. Maybe he's sleeping with his eyes open." He moved behind Nika.

Past the cougar cage was a smaller cage with foxes in it. One of them was almost black. They were splotchy and skinny, not like storybook foxes. They paced constantly back and forth with a smooth gliding motion, wheeling around when they got to the corner. Thomas squatted down to talk to them. Instead of stopping, they ducked away, their gaze sharply focused on something in the distance. Nika followed their gaze. Nothing was there except a rocky field and some dead grass. *Maybe they were looking at freedom,* she thought.

They could see other pens behind the first two. In one was a flash of black and white. In another, four raccoons were pressed together in a small cage. They lowered their heads, staring from the shadows.

When one of the raccoons hissed, Nika said, "Let's leave."

"You kids get outta here," a voice growled from behind the cougar's pen, making all three jump. They hadn't heard any footsteps. They turned and froze, as a man walked slowly toward them. He had a shaved head, a long untrimmed beard, and a dirty shirt that puckered between too-tight buttons.

It was the swearing man she'd seen off Big Berry Island. As in a bad dream, Nika wanted to run, but her muscles turned to rubber. She lowered her head, hoping the man wouldn't recognize her. Randall grabbed Nika's arm, and Thomas bravely stepped forward with a cautious smile.

"We just came to see the animals. It's a nice cougar." Clearly Thomas had learned the value of a little conversation at the right moment.

The man put his head back and laughed, a rusty barking sound. "Nice, you think? Yeah? I bet he'd like to *eat* one of you. That's if his teeth were still good." His laughter turned into deep coughs. He turned around and spat on the ground.

Thomas was slowly stepping backward and bumped into Nika and Randall.

"What about that wolf you had, the tan one?" Thomas asked.

The whites of the man's eyes showed as his stare drilled into Thomas. He snapped a glance at Nika. A question flicked across his face.

"Too much trouble. I thought she'd make pups. With him." He pointed to a large black dog lying alone in a cage beyond the foxes.

Nika noticed one cage with its gate open.

"Good money for pups like that. But that tan bitch, she dug out, the worthless bag of bones." He swore a long string of words. When he finished, he had a confused, faraway look on his face. Then he seemed to get angry again, his eyes on the empty cage.

"You kids deaf? Now get!" His eyes darted around almost as though he were seeing something. Then he turned and walked to the windowless shed, going in and slamming the door behind him.

They turned and ran, hearing the cough-scream one more time, just before they hit the road at edge of his property.

Only when they were back on Roosevelt Street did they talk again. Thomas tried to laugh, but his voice sounded wobbly. "What a nutcase!" he said, breathing hard.

Nika slowed to catch her breath. But she was still scared. Was this the man who stole Khan's brothers and sisters? Why was he keeping animals like that? It didn't make sense.

Walking beside her, Randall's eyes were so big and his skin so white that she put her arm around him. With a shift of his thin shoulders, he slipped from her arm and moved closer to Thomas, where he matched his steps to the longer steps of the bigger boy. Was he mad at her? She really didn't understand Randall lately.

For a minute she stopped on the sidewalk and let them get ahead of her. Then she turned around and glared back toward Bristo's. She wanted to shout at him. He had no right to cage wild animals. It certainly seemed like the authorities weren't doing much. But maybe there was something she could do. She looked at Thomas striding ahead, remembering that he could drive a boat.

The silvery-tan wolf pulled herself up on the rocks of the small island. Standing on the shore, she shook, water spraying first from her head, then from her body, finally from her tail. She stood to listen. There were no frightening sounds. She heard the sound of wings. The wolf slipped into a shaded area on a rise where she could rest and see. As she lay down, the dry lichen crunched beneath her. She tasted wildness in the air.

Chapter Nine

When Nika saw Lorna sitting on a chair with Khan nowhere in sight, she narrowed her eyes in frozen anger. She cleaned her shoes, then stood beside the doorway to wait for Ian.

"Oh, you're back!" Lorna closed her magazine. Her smile abandoned one side of her mouth.

Ian appeared beside Nika, cleaned his shoes, and walked into the porch. "Where's the pup?" he asked, glancing around. He leaned over to look into the kennel.

"He isn't very tame, is he?" Lorna threw her hands up in an exasperated gesture.

Nika rolled her eyes.

"Anyway, what happened was, well, first I tried to get

him to snuggle, or eat. I tried to play with him, but he kept creeping away. I tried to hold him to make him eat, but he snarled and ran into the kennel. When I pulled him out, he snapped."

A flame of *told you so* burned in Nika's eyes as she glared at Ian.

"Anything else?" Ian asked. His foot was tapping the floor.

"Later I accidentally knocked over my empty pop can, and I guess it clattered. Anyway, that's when he squeezed behind there." Lorna pointed to the den box, a crestfallen look taking the place her smile. She stood with her arms wrapped around herself.

"Thanks, Lorna, but maybe you should go into the kitchen for now, until we get him out." Lorna stepped over the baby gate into the house, shrugging. Ian got down on his knees and carefully eased the wooden den box out a few inches.

"I see him," said Ian. "Hey, Mr. Khan. Hey, pup."

Nika walked quietly across the porch to her sleeping bag and sat down cross-legged, pulling the floppy bear next to her. "Hey, Khan, hey, little one, here, puppy, pup. Come here, Khan-boy." She waited. She wondered if the next time Lorna came, Khan would be afraid of her, if he would remember her smell.

"Here, puppy pup, here, Khan-boy, here, pup-pup," repeated Ian, making lip-squeak noises.

A sleepy pup slowly crawled from behind the kennel, step by step. Ian moved to give him room. Khan stretched and looked around, then skittered over to Nika's bag, where he tried to squeeze between her back and the knee wall. She reached behind and stroked the soft folds of his ears and kept talking gently, "Good boy, Khan, good pup." After a few minutes he backed out, crawled over her leg, and fell into her lap, where he settled, lowering his head on her knee. She wanted to pick him up and hug him, but she didn't. Better to let him choose his moves. She reached over and placed the red lobster toy in front of him. He grabbed one of its legs and gave it a ferocious headshake. Ian said headshaking was a predatory skill wolves needed as adults, that a shake could snap the necks of small prey. After working over the lobster, Khan showed more confidence and jumped from her lap. He ran back and forth, relieved himself, then came back and climbed on top of the stuffed bear, kneading it with his paws.

"Hungry boy, huh, pup?" Nika got up, cleaned up his puddle, noted it on the chart, then climbed over the baby gate. She set some water on the stove to heat, keeping an eye on Lorna, who was busily explaining to Ian something about her uncle's dog and how it bit people. The girl was a ditz, Nika decided. She wondered if Ian would admit he'd made a mistake in trusting her.

o o o

After dinner that night, Ian bugged Nika to get to work on the pup report she was supposed to write for school credit. He told her he'd watch the pup. So she spread out on Pearl's big table, with note cards and the giant stack of Ian's well-worn books and articles. She wrote that the "transition period" was over now and that Khan was starting the "socialization period"—the time, at about three weeks of age, when wild wolf pups first stick their noses out of the den. He weighed 5.2 pounds, and his hearing was beginning to develop. His ears were beginning to stand up. If he growled or snapped at someone, Ian and Nika quickly distracted him with a piece of food or a toy. He liked to hide under his stuffed bear with just his back legs sticking out.

A few days later Nika shared her idea with Thomas, and they made a plan. He got permission to take the fishing boat and they agreed to meet at the Camerons' in the morning. Randall was mad at Nika for not including him, but she said something lame about how she missed Olivia and Zack and that she needed time with someone her own age. (Both true, really.) Randall had fired off a glare, marched back into the boys' cabin, and slammed the door. Nika knew that he must be especially furious with her for horning in on his fishing time with Thomas. But she was really protecting Randall. It was enough that she and Thomas were going to cross a line.

It was a perfect glassy-water morning when Thomas came puttering around the point in his small fishing boat powered by a 9½ horsepower motor. They loaded nets and poles to make it look like they were going to fish and headed toward Red Pine. The boat steadily worked its way across the calm surface of the lake, cutting through the shreds and layers of mist that peeled off the water like curtains lifting on a stage. As the motor hummed along, she could tell it was going to take longer to get to town than it had in Ian's fast boat.

Before they tiptoed up to the skunks' cage, Thomas told her, "Bristo drinks a lot, so he probably wouldn't wake up this early even if a land mine went off in the yard."

The wire cutters they'd borrowed from the Camerons' toolshed were dull, and cutting turned out to be much harder than they'd expected. When they'd finally cut a jagged hole just big enough for the skunks to escape, Thomas whispered, "Don't worry, they're fixed, so they won't squirt us." They knelt to watch. It wasn't long before skunks slipped out, shimmying silently into the brush behind the cages, holding their tall tails high like flags, their butts swaying back and forth.

Next they went to work on the fox pen. The foxes stopped their pacing and slouched in surprise. They jerked back whenever Nika or Thomas moved. This time Thomas cut a flap in the wire and tied it open. When they stood back to watch, two very thin, splotchy red foxes crept up to examine the hole. One squeezed out, then another, followed by the blackish one. Soon they were quick shadows flicking through the trees.

The raccoons seemed very tame, coming up close to the fence while Nika snipped the wire. Their coats were matted and dull. When they finished, four raccoons jammed through the hole in close single file and hunched away into the trees. The dog barked hoarsely when they got close to his cage, so they threw him a handful of dog biscuits that Thomas had thought to bring and hurried to the enclosure holding the cougar. The dog stopped barking long enough to eat the biscuits but continued to growl and follow them with his eyes.

Nika's hand cramped as she clamped the wire cutters on the chain link of the cougar's cage. She wasn't sure she could cut it. She laid the clippers down to rest her hand. Hesitating, she looked at the animal and listened to its gravelly breathing. It was so big. They hadn't thought much about how it might hurt them. Nika watched the cat's twitching tail tip and motionless eyes.

Thomas said, "It doesn't really look like it wants to leave, does it?"

Tail twitch. "Either that, or it's getting ready to attack," answered Nika. "Besides, it's old, isn't it? Look how its ribs stick out." Just then the cougar showed them that it might be old, but it could still lunge and make a nasty snarl. They both jumped and ran.

When they stopped, Nika's hands were shaking. "Scary, huh?" she managed to say.

Thomas nodded, wiping sweat from his face. "Can you believe we were dumb enough to think that cougar might just stroll off into the forest?" He thumped his head with one hand.

"At least not so dumb as to actually cut the wire," Nika said weakly. Soon both of them were laughing and making cougar snarls at each other.

When they looked back, the cougar was on the roof of the lean-to again. As they walked through the alleys of town, they heard it cough-roar several times. The sound kept them moving quickly toward the dock.

As Thomas's boat chugged out into the lake, he steered it around Eagle Island, heading for the nesting tree. They looked at each other, but neither spoke. When they could see the nest, Thomas cut the engine and they drifted, lying back on the seats, staring silently at the flat blue sky and the smooth reflecting lake.

Letting out a breath that was half laugh and half gasp, Thomas said, "Those foxes really moved! And those raccoons waddled like old ladies. I hope the skunks do okay without their sprayers . . ."

"They're all free!" said Nika.

They both sat up, reached over, and high-fived.

"Oh, look, one of the eagle parents is coming with food," she said, pointing. "See the chicks' heads poking up?" They sat in the gently rocking boat watching as one eagle landed and proceeded to rip the fish apart and stuff bits into reaching beaks.

Thomas leaned forward and tapped Nika's arm. "Look, did you see that?" He pointed into the woods beneath the nest. "I saw something move. Right under the eagle's nest. Funny, nobody comes out here except to dump fish remains."

Nika turned her head and looked at the rock slabs and dense shrubs and their mirrored reflections in the lake. "I don't see anything. Maybe it was a squirrel."

"Big squirrel." Thomas laughed. He looked for a while longer, then pulled the starter on the outboard, aiming the boat back toward home.

Nika felt the breeze on her face. She felt pleased with what they'd done. Those animals didn't deserve to live like that. Now they were free. And they'd gotten back at Bristo for snatching pups and imprisoning animals. It served him right.

"Hey, Nika, let's remember to put the wire cutters back, okay?" shouted Thomas over the motor noise.

"Yeah, okay." She remembered dropping them by the cougar's cage. She must have picked them up. "Just a sec, I'll check my backpack." She dumped all of the contents of the bag onto the bottom of the boat. "I don't see them. Are you sure you don't have them?"

"No. You had them last."

"Oh, well, it doesn't matter, does it? No one will ever go behind that cage. I guess they're lost."

"Are you sure?" Thomas asked loudly. His forehead wrinkled. She put up her hands.

As the boat gained speed, they looked at each other and shrugged. It was too late to go back. They could pool their money and buy another pair for Thomas's dad.

Releasing the animals felt good. In a way, it was like setting herself free. Nika loved that the foxes could now run and run through the damp earthy smells of the forest.

But by the next week, the secret about Bristo's animals became heavier to carry. It wasn't that they told a lie. No one even asked them if they'd caught fish on their supposed fishing trip. But it felt like a lie. When they planned it, she had been sure they were doing the right thing, but now the secret stuck in her throat. She found it hard to look at Ian when he talked to her, so she avoided conversation, except about pup care and dinner and the loon calls at night. She wasn't sorry about what they'd done, but she couldn't figure out why she felt so alone. Thomas seemed to be busy all the time helping his dad build a deck. Added to that, Randall was still mad at her.

For Nika the best part of every one of the following days continued to be Khan. One thing was certain—he liked her best. With everyone he met, except Lorna, the pup was friendly and relaxed, but when a sound scared him, he ran to Nika. When others were in the porch, he eased onto her lap to look at them. And when she was with him, touching his springy undercoat, rubbing his oversize feet, she felt whole in a way that she hadn't felt since her mom died.

Nika settled into her pup care schedule, and the days ran together. She couldn't believe how big and agile Kahn was becoming. His legs got longer. His ears got taller, though the tips still flopped over now and then. Ian showed her how to make gruel for Khan, mixing formula, vitamins, and ground meat together to the consistency of lumpy oatmeal. Khan ate it from their open hands rather than a bowl and loved it. Ian said they would be weaning him off the bottle soon. He brought him deer feet and pieces of hide to drag about and use for teething. One nice thing about all of the quiet time with Khan is that she finished all of her homework, except science. And they had given her until fall to finish the pup project.

One day Zeus came racing up the path, his sharp

barks announcing Pearl's return. Nika let the dog into the house and watched while he made the rounds of the rooms, then plastered himself against the gate to the porch. Nika was amazed that he didn't seem upset. Instead he stared through the barrier, his tail moving in little interested twitches.

"Well, I guess it's dangerous for me to go away for very long." Pearl came through the front door with a smile and dropped her travel bags on the living room couch. "Things happen." She reached to hug Nika. Ian followed, carrying more of Pearl's things.

"So let's see this little fellow."

Nika led Pearl to the screen porch and put her hand down to open the baby gate.

"What about Zeus?" Nika asked Ian.

"I think it's about time to introduce Khan to another canine. We'll just watch carefully. The little wolf could use some dog-style bossing around."

Nika swung back the gate, and Zeus trotted straight to the wooden box and sat down. Ian, Pearl, and Nika all tiptoed into the porch and waited. When Khan staggered out, unsteady from sleep, he crab-stepped sideways up to Zeus and started licking the older dog's chin, then curled down on his back in front of him. Zeus straightened his tail and stood tall, as tall as a small dog can stand. The pup rolled and licked at his chin again. Zeus made little darting lunges at the pup, pushing him down. Every time the pup came back wiggling and whining and low-wagging his tail. It was a long time before Khan even noticed the humans in the porch.

Nika smiled at Pearl. Communication between these canine cousins was not going to be a problem.

As they were watching the pup and the small dog, Ian said, "When I was in town picking you up, Pearl, I heard some news about Bristo. Remember I mentioned he might have stolen three-three-two's pups?"

"Yes. Yes, I do."

Nika's eyes froze on the dog playing with the pup in the straw. Her breath caught. She waited.

"He's been rampaging around town, drinking too much, shouting and carrying on about how the government had really done it this time. They locked him up a couple of days ago, just to get him sober. Fencing was cut, most of his animals escaped, and he was going on about it."

"Poor man," Pearl said.

"Right after we found number three-three-two, I made a call to Erv Dunn, the new sheriff, and he made a trip to check for pups at Bristo's place. He didn't find anything. At that time all the other animals were still there. Erv went back yesterday, and all the cages were empty, except for the one holding the ancient cougar."

"What did Bristo do with the wolf pups?" asked Pearl.

"Well, sold them, I suppose, if they survived. We know he's made money on wolf pups before, selling them as pets." Ian looked serious. At least he didn't say anything about wire cutters, or kids, or anything like that, Nika thought.

But she'd heard enough. She wished Ian would stop talking.

Ian continued. "In jail, Bristo has been muttering about some 'wolf bitch' and how she'd be sorry. When they arrested him, he was leaning against a Dumpster on Main Street, ranting. He was holding an empty rifle and a pair of wire cutters."

"It's too bad," Pearl said. "He needs help. Many people have tried, but he always runs them off."

Wire cutters. Nika felt a squirmy feeling in her stomach. But she couldn't feel sorry for Bristo.

A silence fell as they watched the pup pounce and wrestle with Zeus.

Pearl got up and started into the kitchen, "I brought some special ground meat from the butcher," she said. "Leftovers from meat cutting with lots of finely ground bone in it. It should be good for Khan's gruel. We'll let Zeus have a little, too."

"Nika, do you want to try giving him some?" Ian was looking carefully at Nika.

Suddenly she was on her feet. "I'll get a bowl. Shall I get some formula, too?" She asked in a chirpy voice. But for a minute, her feet were riveted to the floor.

"Darling, what is it?" asked Pearl.

"Nothing," Nika said quickly and headed toward the kitchen.

At least Bristo was in jail. Maybe they would keep him there.

The wolf explored the island, chasing snowshoe hares in brown summer coats as they zigzagged through dense trees. She found bits of fish dropped by eagles. Every day she paced the shoreline, then circled to her lookout rock. She felt constant hunger, but she could wait. The days were warmer. Fingers of cool air slipped down the rock as the late sunset simmered at the horizon. The silvery-tan wolf curled tightly and lost herself in sleep.

Chapter Ten

Khan loved the bone-dust meat from the butcher. They mixed it with vitamins and formula in a small plastic bowl. At forty-two days he weighed eighteen pounds. Some days he gained a whole half a pound. Ian told her that it was time to stop giving him a bottle, but she thought that if he still wanted it, why not? She loved the moments when his gangly body stretched across her lap sucking the formula down in a few strong pulls. Would his wild wolf mom have just turned off the taps one day and said, that's it?

She did know from her reading that this was the age when wolf parents would bring back partially digested food in their stomachs. Pups licked at their mouths and they would regurgitate. So if Khan had been wild, he would have been eating vomit! "If you think I'm going to eat this first and then throw it up, you're wrong," she told him as she offered the gruel. Khan still preferred to eat it from the cup of her hand. He was always careful with his needle teeth, licking and nibbling the food delicately, not missing a single sticky bit.

One night a thunderstorm shook the island. Nika felt the floor vibrate, watching cords of lightning crisscross the sky. The plastic had been removed from the screen porch, so they lowered the heavy canvas shades. In the morning, however, every item in the porch was damp. Her clothes and her sleeping bag sponged up humidity from the air.

That morning after feeding, Nika sat watching the pup ferociously shake one paw of the stuffed bear. When Ian came through the barricaded gate from the house, he laughed at Khan. "By the way, it's about time for our growing pup to try the outside world. Zeus's small fenced yard will be perfect for his first adventures. Before long we'll have to build something more secure." Ian had already put up plywood barricades, leaving the screens open just at the top. The porch was not exactly people-usable anymore, but Pearl didn't seem to mind.

It bothered Nika how things were beginning to change. It had been so nice when Khan was tiny and the screen porch had been a snug den for just the three of them.

"Are you sure it's not too soon for him to go outside?" she asked.

"In the wild he would have been outside before now. He's six weeks old. It's past time." Ian turned away.

She wondered if Ian would miss those first days with Khan as much as she would. Maybe for him it was just a job.

Nika and Zeus led the way into the small fenced yard. Khan followed cautiously, but when he stepped on a stick and it snapped up and hit him on the nose, he raced back into the porch with his tail tucked.

"He's scared," Nika said.

"Wolf pups are all about being scared and fleeing to safety," Ian explained. "It's a good way for them to stay alive. That's why it's necessary to socialize pups when they're only a couple of weeks old. If they're older than that, fear usually wins. But curiosity is strong, too. Give him time."

It didn't take Khan long to creep on bent legs back out of the porch and into the fenced area. He sniffed every inch of bare rock and mossy ground, the sticks, the stumps, and the early grasses. In one corner next to a large white pine, the ground was thick with needles. Khan dug with his front paws and settled beneath this tree. Soon he dug some more, eagerly opening a hole between two outstretched roots until it was big enough to curl down into. Lying in the hole, his woolly black coat filled with dirt and needles, he watched the woods beyond, his ears twitching to small sounds.

"He likes it," Nika said from her perch on a stump in the middle of the yard. "Look, Ian, his ears are standing up completely now, wolflike."

"His ears are open now, too, so he can hear pretty well." Ian sat on a taller stump and tapped the ground with a branch of balsam he'd broken off. Khan leaped up, sidestepped, then ran in jerky dashes until he grabbed the branch. Ian released it, and Khan ran with it, shaking and finally throwing it over his shoulder.

"He looks happy," Nika said. "Do wolves have emotions?'

"Not like ours. They seem very emotional with each other, but we don't really know how animal feelings work. There are some good books on the subject."

Nika gently distracted the pup from chewing on her shoes by dragging a mangled piece of hide in front of his nose. She had learned from Ian that shoe-chewing and other biting on humans had to be discouraged. When instructing her, Ian had shown her a moose thighbone as big around as her arm. Then he told her how Khan's powerful jaws would be able to bite through that thighbone in six to eight bites when he was grown. She got the picture.

"How come he's so black?" Nika asked. Before meeting Khan, Nika had always pictured wolves as being mostly gray.

"Remind me to give you the article for your report, but DNA research suggests the black phase wolves came from being crossed with wild dogs as long as ten to fifteen thousand years ago. Dogs came from wolves, now they say black wolves came from dogs!"

Ian stood and headed toward the house. "Nika, I forgot to tell you. At the end of the week I'm going down to St. Paul for an important meeting. Pearl will be here with you while I'm gone. I've lined up people from the college in Red Pine to take shifts with the pup. Elinor, a new researcher who's just joined my study, will be in charge."

Things were moving too fast. The yard. St. Paul. New people. Someone named Elinor?

"Remember how we talked about making a large fenced run for Khan? So he can explore and really run?"

Nika nodded.

"I've been thinking about the clearing up on the ridge, just beyond those trees edging the house." He turned to point up the hill. "An old cabin used to be there. It burned down a long time ago. Anyway, it would give Khan a pretty open area to run and burn off some energy. The ground is rocky, so we wouldn't have to worry so much about him digging out along the fences. It's an easy walk from the house for helpers. It'll just be temporary . . ."

And then what? Nika thought but was afraid to ask. She looked at the pup as he curled at her feet, his head resting on her shoe.

"We can teach him to walk on a lead to go up and back," Ian said.

"He'll follow." She felt certain of that.

"Maybe. Maybe not." Ian gave her a long look, both hands in his back pockets. "Anyway, on Friday several guys I know from forestry are coming. They'll make short work of the fencing. Elinor's coming with a couple of pup volunteers, to get to know you and Khan." He headed into the porch.

"Not Lorna, I hope." Nika scooped up Khan from where he'd fallen asleep and carried him back into the porch, where she placed him in his den box. He groaned and stretched his long legs. She touched his ears and mouth and paws for a few minutes. It was one of the things Ian suggested they do so when the vet needed to handle him when he was older, he could. Now she had to let other people handle him, too.

She sat beside the den box drenched with Khan's puppy smells and watched Ian step over the baby gate. He hadn't really said anything about taking Khan away from here. Her mind clouded at this point. She needed to know more, go to the library, look on the Internet. Maybe she could keep Khan, if she had a special fenced area, even in California? An ache filled her, and she tried to sweep away the inner warnings about not getting her hopes up.

By Thursday Khan was enjoying playing chase with Zeus around their small yard. But by Friday it was already clear he needed more space. He had grown another half pound as well. The crew came early that morning, and the hill pen was finished by dinner, complete with logs holding the bottom of the fencing to keep Khan from digging out.

Pearl rewarded the volunteers with lunch. Everyone talked at once, and their voices filled the open room. Nika helped serve platters of roast beef and cream cheese sandwiches, fresh salad and raw veggies, cold sweet potato fries, and pitchers of iced tea. When all of the food was on the tables, she headed for the kitchen.

"Don't you want to join us?" Ian called after her. Pearl sat down with the crew, sharing in their laughter.

"That's okay," Nika answered, and waved a sandwich in the air.

Standing in the kitchen, she ate quickly. She didn't want to carry human food when she went to see Khan.

Ian came to the kitchen door. "Wait on feeding Khan," he said. "I want Elinor to give him the meat today, and Will and Abby, the two volunteers from the college, will watch. Elinor is going to give them an orientation about wolf pup development. Okay?"

Nika turned to look at him and nodded, but he was already heading back to join the others at the table. It was hard to believe, but here it was, turning out just as she feared. Let the kid play with the pup for a while, then the adults take over. She hardly knew what to say. Maybe this Elinor knew stuff from books, but why didn't Ian ask *her* to show the college kids how to care for Khan? She knew Khan. Her feelings of trust for Ian had started to sprout small pale roots, but now they felt like they'd been ripped from the ground.

Avoiding the crowd at the table, Nika went over the gate and through the porch to the screen door leading outside. Khan was lying on the tattered stuffed bear. "C'mon, little one. Let's go, pup. Hey, puppy, pup . . ."

The pup looked at her with interest, pulled to his feet, and followed her to the door. She opened it, and they crossed the small dog yard. "Now. Let's go see the new fence," she said, quietly, opening the gate out of the yard. She had grabbed a strip of raw deer hide from the freezer and now held it out for him.

Nika jogged up toward the new hill pen, holding the hide behind her and looking over her shoulder. Khan followed, stopping to sniff the trail a few times, then racing to catch up. A path well packed by the forestry crew led up to the open spot on the hill. She ran through the new gate, then turned to wait for Khan, tossing the hide. He chased, pounced on the hide, shook it fiercely back and forth, then carried it around the new enclosure, running faster than she'd ever seen him run before. After several loops at high speed, he found a large flat rock, jumped up, and settled to chew the hide. Nika closed the gate and fastened the latch. Watching him run was a thrill. She always loved being with him, but watching him run like the wind was a whole new level of happiness. It was as though he already knew inside what it was to be a wolf.

The new larger pen was about the size of four living rooms and had shade, rocks, and room to run. They'd put a child's wading pool in one corner, the kind with a pull drain in the bottom. Just outside the fence was a hose with a trigger nozzle. Rocks surrounded the wading pool.

They could just come up here and find us, Nika decided. She sat down cross-legged inside the pen, leaned against the trunk of a large white pine, and waited.

Khan's straight-up ears rotated like satellite receivers. His hearing was definitely online. Nika turned to look toward the path. Ian led the way, walking stiffly, hands fisted in his pockets. Striding behind him was a redheaded woman with a long braid down her back. She was dressed like Ian, all khaki and boots. She decided this must be Elinor. There was a catlike grace about her that reminded Nika of the way Olivia moved. Olivia, whose favorite thing was modern dance. A young man and a young woman followed behind them, grinning like kids happy to be asked along on an adventure. She'd hardly noticed them at lunch, she'd been so eager to get out the door. The young man was tall and loose-jointed and held his head at an angle as if he were waiting for the answer to a question. The young woman was solid, not fat, but looked rooted to the earth by her sturdiness. She had a bush of dark brown curls escaping from a baseball cap that said, "Earth Is Home." Nika had to admit that they both looked okay.

Nika stayed braced against the tree. Khan ran and stood beside her, his eyes on the newcomers. They entered, and Ian closed the gate. Then he bent down and called, "Here, Khan-boy, here, pup." Khan twisted his small black body and ran to him, his tail circling, his head low. He rolled in front of Ian and got a proper belly rub. Standing, the pup cast uncertain glances toward the three who squatted down against the fence. Then, he ran a circle toward the others and returned to energetically cover Ian's face and ears with toothy licks. Elinor called Khan's name. Before long he walked over to investigate, sniffing one person at a time. He licked Elinor's face, then poked behind her for the bowl of meatball treats. She held one out to him. He stretched his body, took a meatball, dropped it, then raced across the enclosure to Nika again. *Hah!* Nika thought. So much for the fancy research assistant and her meatballs.

But Elinor didn't give up. She crooned, "Here, Khan, come here, boy, good boy, here, pup. Here, Khan-boy."

She held out her hand again. Khan made a second approach. This time he gently slid the meatball from her hand, then took a few steps away before gulping it down. Elinor smiled and laughed. "What a cautious little wolf you are." Reminding the two volunteers to let Khan approach them, she handed the bowl of meatballs to the young man. Soon Khan had taken treats from everyone until he'd had enough and went off to watch them from his new rock throne.

Ian got up from where he had been sitting and walked over to Nika. For a moment he just looked at her, his brows pushed together in a question. She stood.

"So how did it go, coming up here?" he asked.

She tried to decide if he was mad or not. It was hard to tell. He wasn't smiling, though. "Oh, perfect." She brushed off her jeans. "He came right along with me. He was great."

"Well, good, and at his age, following is natural." Ian folded his arms over his chest. "But just be sure two people are on a shift when he's transferred back and forth from now on. Use a leash. Carrying still works. We wouldn't want to lose him after all of our hard work."

So it was shifts now, like at a fast food place. But she knew Khan would stay with her. She wouldn't lose him, ever. Besides, they were on an island. "Yeah, okay," she said, watching the volunteers admire Khan as he dragged the chunk of deer hide around the pen.

o o o

The next morning Nika awoke in the screen porch as she heard Ian getting ready in the kitchen. She peeked at the clock they'd hung high on the wall. Five-thirty a.m. She shut her eyes again. Ian whispered goodbye to her, and then the sounds of his footsteps drummed across the living room.

Khan was still asleep under the stuffed bear. After she knew Ian was gone, Nika got up and went into the kitchen. A note was taped to the counter: YOU KNOW THE DRILL WITH THE PUP. BE SURE TO VISIT RANDALL. TELL PEARL WHERE YOU ARE GOING. START TYPING THE PUP HOMEWORK PROJECT ON THE COMPUTER. TAKE CARE MOVING THE PUP TO THE HILL PEN. I MADE A SCHEDULE FOR VOLUNTEERS, 2 PEOPLE AT A TIME, 8 HOURS ON. ELINOR HAS 4 MORE VOLUNTEERS FROM THE COLLEGE. HAVE FUN. SEE YOU SOON. IAN.

Not exactly a warm and fuzzy note. But studying the details and the neatly written schedule posted on the kitchen cabinet, Nika realized that volunteers were lined up for the evenings and Elinor was only coming every other day. On the opposite days, Nika and Pearl would be completely in charge. That started Nika thinking about an outing she'd begun to dream about. Something that maybe now she could really do.

The silvery-tan wolf ate, but it was never enough. Emptiness kept her moving. Always before with the woman, and then the man, food had come to her. Now her instincts sharpened and she hunted mice and voles. Stiff-legged, the wolf pounced at small fish in the shallows.

Chapter Eleven

Two days after Ian left for St. Paul, Nika decided that today was the day to take Khan for a run on the Big Island. The night before she imagined how it would be, like Julie and Amaroq in *Julie of the Wolves*. The way Ian talked, the pup would never be able to live like a wild wolf. But she wanted Khan to smell and feel the spaces and freedom of the forest.

After a restless night, Nika took Khan from the porch to the hill pen and gave him his meat mixture. Then she came back down to find Pearl. Pearl had said that she was fine with Nika spending today alone with Khan, but still Nika was nervous about her plan. Two new volunteers were lined up to stay tonight with the pup, and she didn't know exactly what time they were coming. She would have to be home before anyone found her and Khan Missing in Action.

After stuffing a cheese sandwich and an orange for herself and meatballs for Khan into her backpack, Nika called, "Pearl!" She found Pearl in her studio off the living room.

She was painting. Pearl had always illustrated her husband's books and articles. Now that he was gone, she still painted northern plants and flowers, animals and trees. Pearl looked up. "Everything okay out there?" She smiled and put down her brush.

Nika walked closer. A half-done painting of a moose up to his knees in a pond stood on the easel.

"I love your painting. It's so watery. But real, too."

"Some rainy day I'll teach you," said Pearl. "So what are your plans for today?"

Nika tried to line up her words. She wanted to tell the truth, just not *all* of it. "Well, I thought I would take food and some books for my project and just spend the rest of the day with Khan. I'll be back for dinner." She shifted her loaded backpack to her other shoulder.

"Fine, dear. I'll come up around suppertime, and we can bring Khan down together. Those young volunteers are coming."

"Yeah, I know. Have a nice day. 'Bye!" Nika went through the coolness of the house and out through the screen porch and up the path.

Her stomach felt jittery as she approached the gate. Khan greeted her with his whirling dance, licking and jumping. When he settled down, she opened the gate again and said, "Come, Khan-boy, come, puppy pup, come now . . ." and she trotted to a path that went directly down to the sand spit from the old cabin site. As though Khan did this every day, he trotted along with her, stopping to sniff now and then. He stayed close to her as they approached the sand spit and the inlet. He drank from the lake and started to chase a minnow, so she scooped him up and carried him quickly across the sand spit up to where the woods path split from the main trail. She didn't want to spend much time visible on the beach. Up the woods path about fifty feet, she put the squirming pup down.

Then she jogged slowly along the trail, calling to the pup now and then. He stayed with her the whole way. When she stopped at a small shady clearing above the beach cove, Khan lay down in the shade, panting. "This will be our rendezvous spot, like wild pups have," she told him.

Her heart pounded, and she took deep breaths. She couldn't believe what she had done. The pup had followed her. And he liked it. She felt something well up inside, strength, a wildness, a new sense of being alive. A sense of freedom, like none of the hard things in her past could reach her now. She imagined being with Khan on this spot ten thousand years ago, before airplanes and California, before cabins and books and accidents. She might have been dressed in animal skins. They would have smelled the smells and heard the birds call in a steady rhythmic music of trills and twitters and whistles. They would have hunted side by side and slept in skin tents and helped the family.

The day went by quickly. The weather was perfect, not hot, not cold. Even the insects that had been so bad earlier in the summer were less irritating. Squadrons of blue and neon-green dragonflies stitched through the air like tiny silent helicopters, gobbling mosquitoes and black flies. The wind in the trees was like soft breathing.

Khan was teething and found sticks to chew on and drag around. They played in the shallow water of the sand beach. While Khan dug holes, Nika dug out her journal. Then they both fell asleep in the quiet of the afternoon. After waking, Khan came over to her and rolled at her side, letting his feet flop in the air. Even though he was relaxed, his nose twitched and his eyes darted as the ripple of a red squirrel's tale vanished in the leaves above them. Nika rubbed his belly. His guard hairs had begun growing in, making him inky black with tiny sprinkles of gray. His woolly undercoat still showed in dirt-colored patches. She took one of his paws in her hands and massaged the rough pads.

"Good boy, Khan. Good little wolf," she said. The forest breathing with bird song and small breezes felt like home, like what she needed. This place. And Khan. She didn't know why, but here nothing else mattered and she felt peace fold over her like a blanket.

And for no reason she could think of, Nika started to cry.

Khan cocked his head and perked his ears forward as though he was trying to understand this new thing she was doing. Which just made her cry some more.

When she stopped crying, she laughed. She remembered that Meg had called it "raining on the inside" and said it was good for her. Odd, but she had never cried much right after her mom's accident. She'd been numb, like when she cut her hand once on a broken glass in the dishpan. The cut was so deep, it didn't even hurt until after the stitches. The doctor had called it shock. She had felt numb like that after her mom's accident, when she and Randall had been taken to their empty house to pack some things. The first few nights they'd stayed at Olivia's—she kept wanting to go home. She had felt numb all through the nightmare of the funeral, when people talked about her and Randall, offered them food, and looked incredibly sad. She had felt numb when they were taken to the first foster home, where kids fought all the time. She'd felt numb in the second, where it had taken them over an hour on the bus to get to their old school. Then the last one before Meg's. Life became a blur of repacking bags and strange-smelling rooms. Finally they had gone to Meg's, and Nika had started to feel whole again.

Like now. She took in a deep breath and filled her lungs with pine-fresh air.

When the sun was no longer overhead but slanted through the trees in bands, Nika took out the food she'd brought. Khan gingerly ate his meatballs and dragged the hide over to a bed of pine needles. She finished her sandwich and packed the bag again. When Khan was relieving himself, she grabbed his hide and started to jog for home. If they were going to do this regularly, she'd have to create a routine. The game of "keep up" seemed to work. This time he didn't even stop on the sand spit but raced up the hill, sailed through the open gate of the enclosure, and splashed into his pool, where he drank and waded, then lowered in the water to drink again. She'd done it. She'd made her own decision, and everything had turned out fine.

Nika didn't like keeping her run with Khan secret, but when she met Pearl late that afternoon to bring Khan down together, she knew there was no other way. Ian hadn't wanted her even to take Khan up the path to the pen without a leash. If she told Pearl what she'd done, she might never be able to do it again. Maybe after a while she would explain how well it was working, how the pup had stayed right with her, and everyone would understand.

Everything felt different after that first time running free with Khan on the Big Island. It was the third week of June, and the pup was putting on a half-pound to a pound of weight a day. Although it was becoming harder to get him to hold still enough in the sling scale to get his accurate weight. Dave came to give the first vaccinations. Khan was eating mostly meat now and exploring everything, climbing and chewing. The curious pup had begun to damage things in the screen porch so Elinor had decided he should spend his nights in the larger pen from now on. The pup volunteers would bring sleeping bags and spend nights on the ground.

Keeping track of the pup's fast development, Nika rarely thought about Pasadena anymore. When she did remember, it was like a familiar video she kept in a drawer, one she knew she could play whenever she wanted. But more and more, Pasadena seemed almost like another planet. What was real was running back from the outhouse feeling the cool wet slap of dewy grass on her legs, the scents of pine and decayed wood. It was all so different from a smoggy morning in Pasadena, where the air smelled like flowers, dust, fruit, lawn mowers, air scorched by overheated car engines, and sun on pavement.

Here, everything was new and wild.

That week went by quickly. On Friday, Nika traveled through the kitchen and smiled at Pearl, accepting an egg sandwich to take in her backpack. She felt jittery and confident today, as if she were at the beginning of a race, or about to take a test when she knew the answers. Today would be their fifth secret jaunt together to the Big Island. Every time it was better. Khan always stayed right with her. She could hardly wait to go again today.

One day the wolf heard scraping on the rocks. Loud men got out of a boat. After they left, she bent her legs and approached the place where they had been. Heads and parts of fish were piled on the long flat ledge of granite. Eagles dropped down to grab bits of fish. She curled her lips up from her teeth and rushed at the large birds. It was not much, but she ate.

Chapter Twelve

Will and Abby were full of tales about how Khan had slept underneath the stuffed bear again, how he didn't seem to care that most of his rangy black body now stuck out. They showed her digital pictures and reported that he hadn't eaten much, even though they had mixed his favorite ingredients together with ground moose donated by a hunter. They said they didn't get a weight because he wouldn't hold still in the sling scale. Will handed Nika the clipboard with Khan's weight chart and behavioral observations.

"See you on Monday," called Abby as they let themselves out. "Isn't Tuesday the day Ian comes home from St. Paul?"

"Yeah," Nika called back. "See you guys!"

Just three days until Ian was due back.

Khan was exploding with energy today. He ran to the lookout rock in the pen, circled it, and jetted back, his black body plunging into a full-out run. When he finally came to her, he tugged at Nika's shoelaces. She rolled him onto his back with her hand on his chest between his front legs. "No, Khan," she said. Nika had learned to use her hand firmly, like a jaw (a feeble one, compared to a mother wolf, of course). When Khan stopped squirming and submitted, she rubbed his belly, then pulled the leg of a deer from her bag. He grabbed it, leaped to his feet, shook it, and ran with it. There was no meat on it, so it was mostly a toy. After a few minutes of running and flailing the leg, he dug a hole, placed the deer leg in it, and carefully shoveled dirt over one end with his nose, using a quick nodding motion. He looked proud, as though he'd gone to pup school and he was the best in the class at caching.

When Khan seemed to wear down a bit, Nika opened the gate. He flew down the path they always took. Today for the first time she felt a flash of fear as he disappeared from sight. He ran so fast! When she got to the sand spit, he was lying in the water drinking and dipping his nose in up to his eyes, watching a minnow.

"Good boy, Khan pup," she said, making a click sound

with her tongue to attract his attention. He bounded out, shaking off the water from head to tail tip, soaking her. Then they started up the path side by side. Each time they ran together, Nika felt as if she were in a dream, going up a trail in the middle of nowhere with a baby black wolf at her side. How could this really be happening?

When they reached the top of the path, Khan's ears shot forward, and before she could speak, he stretched his lanky body and was gone in seconds, into the heavy growth of shrubs, wildflowers, and young trees. He was more confident now and wanted to explore on his own. He was probably chasing a red squirrel. He'd be back. Nika continued on their usual route to the clearing above the beach. He'd probably get there before she did.

When she reached the rendezvous spot, Nika looked at her watch. It was nine a.m. By ten she was pacing, watching every flicker of light or change in the shadowed green of the woods. Could a baby wolf get lost? From her reading, Nika knew that wolf pups would follow their mom to a rendezvous spot when they were about eight weeks old, where an older pack member would sometimes stay with them like a babysitter. Khan was over ten weeks old. She'd assumed he would return to their spot.

But by ten-thirty she was calling his name every few minutes and talking extra loud so he could hear her voice. Icy fear sent prickles through her body. What if Khan were injured? It was time to go look for him. She pictured Ian coming home from St. Paul and finding the pup missing.

What could be dangerous to the pup on this island? She had no idea. Maybe other wolves, but she didn't know of any. The only other animal she knew of on the Big Island was a bear. Would a bear hurt a wolf pup? Maybe.

Nika decided to howl. She headed back toward the spot where Khan had disappeared, howling the loudest and longest howl she could produce. Ian had told her wolves could hear each other up to six miles away, sometimes up to ten miles over open land, depending on conditions. Was Khan's hearing developed well enough to hear her? She hoped so. Perhaps wind in the trees blocked her feeble human attempts to copy what she'd learned was a pup-locating howl—very high in pitch. She howled from the tops of rocks, from openings in the woods. She hiked in the direction of the Camerons' but didn't want to get too close. Then she headed down to the uninhabited end of the island. She bushwhacked through tangles of raspberry and serviceberry bushes, tripped on downed logs hidden in low-growing plants. When she reached a rocky point on the far end of the island, she sat down and looked across the water. Could he have decided to swim? He might have fallen into a pit. Or maybe someone had set traps on this island. Then there was Bristo and his boat and that thought made her feel worst of all.

She was in a galloping panic as she tried another route back to the rendezvous area. Her howl was now thin and scared-sounding. Trembly. Smells of sweet fern erupted as she crushed them with her boots. She howled and walked, howled and walked. She began to feel fear shutting down her muscles. She stopped to calm herself, then she howled again.

Suddenly, from beyond the trees, she heard an answering howl. She cupped her ears with her hands. Another howl. Khan! But it wasn't Khan, no high-pitched puppy howls and yips—it was too long and low. Then there was a yodel at the end. A person. She heard it again, closer. Could Elinor be looking for them? She decided to walk toward the sound. Even Elinor would be a happy sight right now. She might be mad, but she would help.

Suddenly there was a snapping of branches, and a small dog shot out of the bushes and ran wildly up to her. Zeus! She squatted down to ruffle the little dog's fluffy coat but kept her eyes on the woods where he'd come from.

More crashing, and Thomas emerged, holding a walking stick in one hand, his backpack hanging loosely from one shoulder.

"Thought you might need the cavalry," he said with a lopsided smile. "So I went to Pearl's and borrowed Zeus."

He stood gazing at her, his lean tan body relaxed but

seeming ready to move. Dressed in blue jeans and a white T-shirt, he looked at her from under the visor of his red baseball cap.

"I can't believe this, Thomas! I really messed up." Nika sat back in the undergrowth and held her hands over her eyes.

Thomas remained very still, waiting. Zeus nuzzled her arm.

"How did you know?" Nika asked, uncovering her eyes and patting the small dog.

"Well, let's guess." Thomas took his baseball cap off and slapped it back on again. "Wild howling all over the island. I could even hear it over the wind. And, no offense, not like real wolf howling. More like human-pretending-to-be-wolf howling. I was trying to sneak up on that bear to catch a photo. I was trying to be very, very quiet. Then, howling. On and on. An hour of howling like that, and it didn't take a nuclear physicist to figure out that you'd lost Khan."

"But how did you know I even had him here?"

"I've seen you before. I figured it was kind of a secret, so I just stayed away."

"Can you help me find him?"

"Sure. But next time you bring him, want my advice?"

"Yeah. Well, what?" She felt a little edgy. He was rubbing it in.

"Bring me. More is better."

"So what do you think happened?" Nika smiled at Thomas.

"Probably he ran into something that scared him, like a porcupine, or maybe the bear, and just hunkered down. Maybe Zeus can find him."

Thomas whistled, then called to Zeus, "Where's the pup, Zeus? Find the pup! Find Khan!"

The little dog looked up at the word "find" and immediately did a nosedive into the undergrowth. A wagging black tail above the carpet of green signaled his progress. They scrambled to keep up.

Zeus climbed higher on the island, over lots of downed trees and steep rock hills.

"I never even go up here," Thomas said, breathing hard. "Hold up," he said, "I smell something." He stopped. "Skunk. Now, that is one animal I'd like to avoid."

Even Zeus sat down as if he were saying to himself, *Been there, done that, no way.*

Up higher above the crest of a bare rock face, leaves and branches were shaking. The gurgling croak of a raven came from a tree nearby.

"Uh-oh. Get ready to run," Thomas said, looking downhill at the tangled way they'd come.

"I don't think running is one of our options. Flying, maybe," said Nika, her eyes following his.

Just then Zeus leaped forward into the undergrowth in the direction of the movement.

"No, Zeus, leave it!" shouted Thomas.

But Zeus didn't. There was a stirring of leaves and rustling just out of their sight. Holding their noses, they braced themselves.

"This could be bad," said Thomas.

Zeus came romping out of the undergrowth with Khan right behind him. The smell of skunk floated around Khan in a balloon of tainted air.

"Khan! Khan-boy!" exclaimed Nika, excited at first, then forced to hold her nose. "Oh, brother." She knelt down to briefly greet Khan, wanting him to feel welcome but not wanting to spend a lot of time up close and personal. Her eyes burned from the stench. "It seems to be mostly on his back end, like he decided to get out of there, but too late." Khan whimper-whined and whirled in greeting.

"Pearl knows what to do," Thomas said, beginning the steep descent, hurrying away from the stinky pup.

Nika followed quickly, with Zeus and Khan falling into line.

And Pearl did. She had dealt with this problem many times over the years. She made a mixture of peroxide, baking soda, and dog shampoo and carried it up to the hill pen.

"Better let me do this." She put Khan between her legs with his back end sticking forward, dumped the solution on the smelliest spot, and rubbed it in. "Okay, Nika, look how he loves to grab the water coming out of the hose. Keep spraying him, let him play, then spray him some more, aiming at his backside. If we need to, we'll do it again."

Two hours later the smell was mostly gone, but a trace shadowed Khan, hovering where he rested like a swarm of gnats.

Pearl returned to the house to start dinner. During the whole process she had not asked one word about why Khan had encountered the skunk. While Khan rolled in the dirt and dug in his cooling spot, Thomas and Nika sat across the pen from him, side by side, swatting at mosquitoes.

"Thanks, Thomas," Nika said. Thomas was her first new friend in forever. In some ways she had always felt more comfortable with boys as friends. Olivia felt that way, too. It was one thing they had in common. Boys were more matter of fact, not always thinking about other people's business. And it was nice how they didn't need to talk every minute.

"Thanks for helping," she repeated, tearing up some weeds.

Then as if the idea had dropped from the sky, she said, "Do you think I could ever keep Khan, you know, as a pet, sort of?" It was a question she hadn't dared ask anyone.

"Well, if I were you, I'd want to, for sure. But I don't know—wolves are kind of different, you know. They're cool, but they aren't like dogs. You can't have them in the house or they'll eat your couch. I read that somewhere."

He looked carefully at Nika, then went on. "I wrote a report last year in school about how dogs came from wolves. It's pretty neat." He told her how over a hundred thousand years ago, wolves, scavenging from human camps, began to alert people to other dangers. Humans watched wolves hunt and learned. Wolves ate what people wasted.

"Cool," she said. "They cooperated and sort of tamed each other."

"Those wolves became the first dogs." He'd read that humans had come to North America with dogs. And that dogs and humans maybe even changed each other's brains. He said from those first wolf-dogs, humans bred every kind of dog, to hunt, to work, to be our companions.

"Even Chihuahuas and Great Danes?" Nika couldn't believe all those sizes and shapes of dogs came from those long-ago wolf genes.

"Yup. All of them."

Nika was impressed. Thomas knew a lot. And he seemed to be thinking about her problem with Khan. At least he didn't say flat out "No way."

"Next time we go to the Big Island," Nika asked

Thomas, "will you come with me? You can take pictures, too."

Thomas stood up, shoved his hands into his pockets, and grinned. "As long as you don't howl the whole time, and we stay away from skunks. Anyway, I'll keep your secret, not that it probably is one, anymore."

There was a slap of the screen door on Pearl's porch, then two female voices. Probably Elinor and a volunteer were on their way up to the pen. "This should be interesting," Nika said to Thomas.

The wolf made daily visits to the fish piles. Eagles and turkey vultures circled. Last in line, gulls bobbed offshore. When the wolf arrived, she chased them all away.

One morning after eating from the fish remains, the wolf looked down the shore. She saw a human with a silver box held to his eyes. She circled to watch him from a distance. Later that day several whole fish appeared upon a rock. The wolf ate. Later she found a pink featherless dead bird. Finally the pain in the wolf's stomach did not drive her to pace continuously. She caught a hare. She watched for the human. She watched for the piles of fish.

Chapter Thirteen

On Tuesday Ian was expected home from St. Paul. When Nika came down from her loft on Monday, she heard Elinor talking with a man at the big table. Nika quickly dodged under the log steps into the kitchen.

At the counter, Pearl was holding out to Nika what she called a "walking breakfast." Today it was homemade sausage wrapped in a biscuit.

"Thanks, Pearl. I just thought I should hurry because Thomas and I are going to town so I can do research for that report I'm writing. I don't want to make him wait." She glanced toward the living room. "Who's here?"

"Dr. Dave, talking with Elinor. They checked Khan

after his wild encounter yesterday, to make sure he didn't get nipped anywhere. Luckily, he'd had his shots."

Nika stood stone still and felt her shoulders tighten.

"Don't worry, he's fine. No breaks in the skin."

She hugged Pearl, holding on for a moment, then grabbed an orange from the counter. She wondered if they would tell Ian, and if they did, what would happen.

"I should be back by dinner."

Nika chose not to visit Khan on her way to Thomas's. She hated missing their morning greeting, but today she didn't want to risk meeting Elinor or Dr. Dave on the path. Last night after Elinor pried details out of her about the skunk, Nika had faked a headache and gone to bed. Then she'd listened from the loft as Elinor and the new volunteer took their sleeping bags up to the hill pen for the night. In the middle of the night she heard Khan howl his new lower, stronger howl. Nika wondered if he was howling for her.

The trek over to Big Island felt funny without Khan. She was used to him lacing a black streak through the trees, always looping back to nudge her hand or brush by her on the path.

Thomas was waiting on the dock when she came across the clearing by the cabins. She waved, then jogged up to the boys' cabin to look for Randall. She opened the screen door to find him on the floor with a game spread out. Gideon and Jasper grinned and said hi. Randall looked up for a minute, then down again, giving her a slight backhanded wave.

"We're going fishing with Jake," he said. "We're going in the big boat all the way to the dam. Ian told me he'd come get me tomorrow and I could sleep over." Randall shifted, turning his back. He was still mad that she and Thomas had become friends.

"Okay, little brother. See you tomorrow then." Nika waited for a moment in the doorway to see if he had anything else to say. She heard the smaller boys both say bye in unison.

At the dock, she and Thomas buckled their life jackets, loosened the ropes, and pushed off. Before starting the motor, Thomas said, "I've got a big surprise, later, after the library." Before she could ask anything, he pulled the starter cord. The engine rattled, then droned loudly as Thomas eased the boat into a circle out into the lake and made a straight line for town.

After picking up the mail and sending letters she had written to Olivia and Zack, Nika and Thomas went over one block to the library. The library in Red Pine took up several rooms of a gloomy brick building with polished stone floors. In the biggest room, two computers sat across from each other on a desk.

Nika gathered several books about wolf reproduction and pups. She hoped to take the books home to study, but she didn't have a library card. Since she wasn't going to be here long, it seemed pointless to get one. She walked over to where Thomas was bent over one of the computers.

Reading her mind as usual, Thomas said, "You can take them out on my card. Hang on, though, I have some stuff to do first. Won't be long."

Nika sat down at the second computer to wait, then decided to do a search online. She plugged in three words. Wolf as pet. And waited. Soon the screen filled up with possibilities. Some of them didn't have anything to do with real wolves. She finally found one called, "So You've Always Wanted a Pet Wolf?" That sounded promising. She double-clicked on the link.

- Wolves can eat 2–5 pounds of good meat a day over a lifetime of approximately 15 years. A diet of dog food is not good for them.
- A wolf pup must not fully imprint on humans but needs some canine contact or else all of its social behavior, including natural aggression, will be directed toward humans.
- A pup must spend limited time with other canines, but it must spend 24 hours a day with humans in its first months.
- Pups should have contact with both male and female humans.

- Don't punish wolf pups. Stop them from biting or chewing, gently and firmly, distracting when possible.
- They need a pen that is half an acre at least with an 8-to-10-foot overhung fence, preferably buried 3 feet in the ground.
- They cannot live in houses. They will tear apart couches and furniture out of curiosity and boredom.
- Socialized wolves can still be predatory.
- If you own a wolf, it should be for some educational reason, such as benefiting wolves by teaching about them.

Nika quickly did some math. Eighty pounds of meat a month. Looking up a grocery ad on the computer, she guessed that if meat cost three dollars a pound, it would cost at least $240 a month just for meat, maybe more. Over $2,800 a year just for food, and $44,800 for food for one wolf in its lifetime, if it lived to be sixteen. That was a lot of dog-walking money.

At least they were raising Khan right, twenty-four hours a day with humans at first, having both males and females handle him. And they'd been right about having Zeus around, but if he weren't around, would Khan be aggressive toward her? Somehow she couldn't imagine Khan ever being dangerous. Why couldn't he just stay a pup?

This article worried her. She wondered if Thomas had read it, if that was where he'd learned that a wolf might eat your couch. This was not the information she had hoped for. She could imagine taking Khan to schools and community centers to teach about wolves. But an eight-to-ten-foot-high buried fence was not an average back-yard. Why were wolves so different from dogs? Nika felt her whole world slide sideways.

She wondered about releasing him back to the wild. She didn't want to let him go, but maybe it would be better for him. There were other wolves out there. He could join a pack. She felt a little better with this thought, but not much. She pushed the print button so she could take the article home and read it again.

She looked up two more articles about wolves and wolf-hybrids as pets and skimmed them. They were even more discouraging.

Thomas stood up from his computer across from her. She liked his shy way of moving, certain and smooth.

"Ready?" he asked.

Nika handed her books to him. She wanted to tell him about what she had read, but the words were still circling in her mind.

As they checked out the books, she overheard the librarian say, "I thought you'd already read these, Thomas?"

He shrugged and smiled, then took the books.

So Thomas had been reading about wolves, too.

"You've read these?" Nika asked him as they stopped on the steps outside the library building. "You didn't say before."

"Most of them," he said, then started to run, shouting back, "Beat you to the Busy Bee!"

It wasn't much of a race. Nika dropped her books twice, and by the time she slid into the booth in across from him, he was casually studying the menu.

"Want to split a giant bacon cheeseburger plate with onion rings?" Thomas put his pocket change on the table.

"Sure. With sour cream."

After lunch, they walked down the street toward the docks. "I've got one more thing to do in town," Thomas said. "I'm picking up some stuff at the First Street Market, okay? Just a block over."

When he came out with a half-full grocery bag and they started down to the dock, he said, "Now. Time for the surprise."

There was hardly a ripple on the still lake as Thomas backed the fishing boat away from the dock. He glanced at the overcast sky. "Maybe rain later." Instead of going toward home, he headed left, toward the far point of Eagle Island.

"I knew it! You got some food for the eagles!" shouted Nika over the motor noise.

But Thomas just kept his eyes on the water ahead.

Instead of pulling in beneath the eagle's nest, Thomas only slowed and pointed.

"Forgot my binoculars, but look!" Two brown heads poked up from the nest. They were much bigger now. He kept on going around the point and behind the island. They passed a skirt of rock and were hit by the stench of dead fish. They both held their noses. Halfway down the far side of the island was a little cove where two logs sat half in the water and half out, looking like someone had placed them there. Thomas drove straight toward them and cut the engine. The boat drifted silently between the two logs and came to a halt. He tipped the engine up, scrambled forward, and hopped over the side to pull the boat up.

"Could you hand me the bag?" he asked.

Peeking into the bag, Nika saw pale-colored meat wrapped in plastic. Bag in hand, she climbed over the side and picked her way from rock to rock.

Thomas took the bag in one hand and led her up the ledge to a spot behind some bushy junipers, where he crouched down.

"You stay here. I'll be right back."

Nika watched Thomas move carefully and slowly up until he was at the edge of a dense stand of balsam and spruce trees. There on a level spot at the top of a large rock shelf, he upended his bag. A shrink-wrapped raw turkey fell out. He knelt down to unwrap it, carefully putting the plastic back into the paper bag, which he tucked under his arm. He looked around briefly, then skittered down the rock to sit next to Nika.

"We may have to wait for a while. Here, I brought a pop to share." He pulled a can of root beer from his backpack, snapped it open, and handed it to Nika.

"You're not going to tell me, are you?" she said, taking a drink.

"Nope." He smiled and settled down with his back against a rock.

Nika moved to sit on an oddly twisted white pine trunk, growing out, then up, making a perfect bench with a backrest, like a chair.

"Is it a bear?"

"They like blueberries, not turkey really. Well, I suppose they would, but no. You get three guesses. Two more"

"Is it wild?"

"Yes and no."

"It's both?"

"That's three, you're done. By the way, be very quiet."

It seemed at least an hour that they waited. A loon skidded to a landing behind them, splitting the water into wings of glass. Nika heard the one birdcall that she could identify for sure: the flutelike call of the white-throated sparrow that Pearl taught her that first day. Up note, next note, then dah dada, dah dada, dah. It called from different spots across the island. A painted turtle splashed into the water near the boat and sank like a submarine. Leaves rustled in the tiny breezes weaving through. In the distance they could hear boats coming and going from the town docks. Finally, in the bushes above the rock shelf, there was a whisper of leaves, a crunch of stones.

"Okay. Quiet," said Thomas. Nika hadn't said a thing. She followed the direction of Thomas's eyes.

At first she couldn't see anything, but then she saw two fiery eyes framed in a light shadow among the low bushes where Thomas had dumped the turkey. The shadow floated in front of scraggly trunks of balsam and spruce. The shape of a triangular tawny head emerged slowly. Tall pointed ears. Nika felt the force of the tan wolf's golden eyes as its body pulled slowly from the trees, as smoothly as a dancer. The wolf was so long legged, so tall, so thin. Nika was used to Khan's pup-size body. It stood for a moment, then lightly trotted across the rock to Thomas's gift. It settled with the turkey between its paws and began to eat, bones and all.

"Luna, meet Nika. Nika, meet Luna," whispered Thomas.

"She has a name?" Nika whispered back, trying to restrain her excitement so as not to scare the wolf.

"I named her Luna because she is so pale colored, like the moon. She's the one that ran away from Bristo's, I'm sure of it. She's got a collar. You can barely see it, but it's there. You can see where it has worn away some fur. And she's hungry. She always looks like she wants to come down here, but she never does."

"How did you find her?"

"Remember after we released Bristo's animals, we were sitting in the boat looking at the eagles and I said I saw something? Later I came back with my camera, and I saw her at the fish pile. I wanted to take photos of her, so I followed with my boat till I found this place where she seems to hang out."

"Is she dangerous?"

"I don't think so. Scared, maybe. She always looks curious, like she knows me. I'm beginning to wonder if she belonged to someone before Bristo. Because of the collar. Somehow I can't see her allowing Bristo to put a collar on her."

They watched the wolf eat for a few minutes.

"I suppose she could be a wolf that had been in a study. But the collar isn't fat with a box, like a radio collar."

"They stick out," Nika said. She remembered the collar on the dead wolf.

"I'm worried she can't make it through winter on this island. People dump fish guts, but only in the summer. And once the ice forms, she might go into town looking for food and get into trouble. Or worse, if she goes to town, Bristo might shoot her."

Nika told Thomas about seeing the man in the boat. She was sure it was Bristo now. And Thomas agreed Bristo had probably been looking for Luna. That had been weeks ago.

They were silent for a long time, just watching the wolf eat. When she was mostly finished, she took a chunk of meat up to the edge of the forest, where she dug a hole and shoved dirt with her nose.

"Caching," Thomas said.

"Just like Khan."

On the way home, Thomas drove slowly. He pulled up into a fishing cove, turned off the motor, and anchored. At first they didn't speak.

In a quiet, sad voice, Nika finally said, "I don't think I can keep Khan."

"I know. You must be disappointed."

"But what can I do? He doesn't belong anyplace. I don't know what Ian was thinking when he took him from the den."

"Khan would have died, Nika."

"I know. No, it was right to take him, but I wish we could just let him go again."

"He would probably starve. He doesn't know how to hunt."

They were silent again as small waves made metallic slaps against the side of the boat. The sky was exactly the same gray color as the water. It was as if they were floating in the sky.

"If Luna goes into town, someone will shoot her. We should tell," Nika said. "Who would we tell?"

"They might send her to some wolf rescue place, where they take wolves that people have tried to keep as pets."

"Maybe *both* wolves could live free, together?" said Nika, sitting up. The thought of losing Khan forever wrenched her. But the thought of him having a wild life felt right to her.

"Maybe even have pups!" Thomas smiled.

They high-fived each other. Then unspoken doubts slowed the momentum of their enthusiasm.

"Should we tell about Luna?" Thomas asked.

"Let's not for a while. Ian's back tomorrow. Let's just see what happens the next few days."

"Sure," he said, pulling the cord on the motor.

Now the wolf watched for the two humans to come. She heard the metal scraping, then their voices, gentle and low. She wanted to go to them, to greet them like she had the woman, to roll on the ground nearby. But she remembered the man and the cage, and she stayed behind branches.

Chapter Fourteen

When Nika got home that evening, she took Khan for a short run, returned him to his pen, fed him, then went to bed early. As she stared out the window at stars caught in graceful webs of black branches, she felt the heavy weight of questions. It seemed impossible to figure out what was right for the two wolves.

At times like this her grief hovered in the room like a dark winged creature. She squeezed her eyes shut and remembered Meg saying to her, *Find a favorite memory, and run it through your mind. When you lose someone, you have to find new ways to feel close.* Meg used to say her memories were her jewels to keep forever.

Nika pulled the photo album from her shelf and

found the picture of the three of them around the caterpillar birthday cake Mom made for Nika when she was six. And the one of all of them petting a pilot whale at Sea World. She turned to the ones taken on their trip to Maine. She had just turned ten. Their last trip together. There was a flash picture her mom had taken after she got them out of bed to chase fireflies in their pajamas. Nika remembered feeling the wet grass, laughing, and reaching for the tiny winking lights. On the last page was a photo of her dad in his uniform. She was surprised to see that he looked a little like Ian. She wondered how much they were alike. She had very few memories of her dad. He left her mom shortly after Randall was born to go into the military. She still wished he was in their lives. It always hurt to think of him dying in a munitions accident overseas.

After visiting the photos she felt even more awake. The volunteer hadn't been able to come tonight, and she began to wonder if Khan was lonely. She tiptoed downstairs, grabbed a flashlight and the smelly sleeping bag, and went up the path to the hill pen. When she clinked through the gate, there was no sign of the pup. The stars were so bright, she could see without the flashlight. After lying down in the sleeping bag, she whimper-whined for the pup. He staggered groggily out of the dark and curled his small body on the ground close to her face. He sniffed her closed eyelids, rested his nose on the side of her face with a sigh, then readjusted when his nose slipped off.

After he settled, she gently moved him so he snuggled against the curve of her stomach and folds of the sleeping bag. She felt the thrill of touching his rough fur and listening to his hoarse breathing. Even in the coolness, every muscle in her body relaxed. She had to smile. How many people had slept with a wolf? When she saw the first pale light in the sky, she eased the pup into her warm spot on the sleeping bag and returned to the house.

The next afternoon Ian returned. Pearl came up and spent some time with Nika, watching Zeus and Khan chase wildly around the pen. Nika and Pearl both laughed when little Zeus stood his ground, growling, causing Khan to roll on the ground submissively.

"Khan doesn't realize he's going to be a hundred-pound wolf someday," Pearl said.

"Neither does Zeus."

Nika felt shy around Ian his first night home. Dinner was low key, and she stayed busy helping Pearl. Did he know about her treks to the Big Island and Khan getting lost? What about Bristo? Did he suspect her part in the release of Bristo's animals? After dinner Randall stayed downstairs playing Monopoly with Ian and Pearl until Ian took him back to the Camerons'. Nika decided to go to bed early.

The next morning thin pink light fell in ribbons across Nika's bed. Voices plucked at the fabric of her sleep. From downstairs she heard Ian talking, and the husky sweet voice of Pearl. They spoke in measured, serious tones. Nika slipped from her bed and tiptoed to the top of the stairs. She just heard mumbles, but she felt sure they were talking about her.

That afternoon Ian buzzed over to the Camerons' to fetch Randall and a boatload of his gear for a few days' visit. Nika looked forward to having Randall with her again. Since he had only met Khan briefly as a tiny pup, Randall was thrilled to spend most of the morning in the hill pen, sitting with his back against the fence, watching the pup race and dig. When Khan threw himself onto the ground next to Randall and fell asleep, Randall grinned, waving at Nika and pointing down at the resting pup as she walked around cleaning up scat.

When they came down from the pen, Ian said, "Come on, you two," and led them outside, smiling like he had a big surprise hidden in the woods. He opened the doors of a crawl space tucked beneath Pearl's cabin and plunged into the dark. Soon packs and old dented aluminum pots and pans came flying out.

"Leaving for Russia?" Nika asked.

"No," Ian said, handing her a small ax. "But I thought it was time I took you two on a short canoe trip. Just the three of us."

The pile of packs and plastic containers grew at Nika's feet.

"You know, just being here is kind of like camping already," she said, her voice trailing off.

"Take this tent, will you, Nika?" Ian held out a large green bag. She laid it on the ground with the other stuff. A tent meant sleeping.

Randall bent over, eager to help. Ian handed him a sleeping bag, then another.

"So how does this work? We paddle to a place, camp there, then come home?" Nika was wondering how long she would have to be away from Khan. And Luna.

"Just three nights. Elinor will sleep in my cabin, so she'll be around to watch over Khan. Anyway, the place I have in mind is just a couple of lakes north of here, in the wilderness area. Four short portages in, I know of a great campsite. We can stay there, then fish and explore the lake each day. Here, Randall, can you take these sleeping pads?" Ian pulled himself out of the crawl space and shut the door.

"That's kind of a long time, isn't it?" A hint of a whine threaded through Nika's voice. She imagined a troop of eager volunteers descending on Khan's pen.

"Next is my favorite part—planning the food," Ian said, grabbing several packs and striding back toward Pearl's kitchen.

"S'mores!" Randall shouted, dragging bags on the ground and following.

o   o   o

After seemingly endless hours of measuring portions of biscuit mix, oatmeal, and peanut butter, cutting cheese, labeling plastic bags, and checking off equipment lists, they were finally ready. On the day of the trip, dressed in her shorts and boots and three layers of shirts, Nika ran up to give Khan the meatballs with the vitamins, then raced down to meet Ian and Randall and Zeus at the sand spit. Ian waded into the water in his hiking boots and started loading the canoe.

"Wet foot camping," he announced. After the packs and fishing gear were in, Ian scooped up Zeus and waded out to put him on top. "He loves canoe trips," Ian smiled as the small dog snuggled down between two packs.

Ian held the canoe while Randall waded, then climbed into the center area, his new boots streaming water. Randall sat cross-legged, not even complaining that he sat in a puddle.

"That's called duffing, sitting in the middle. Like a king, the duffer gets to ride," Ian said.

Her hands on her hips, Nika stood motionless on the yellow sand.

In water up to his knees, Ian calmly waited with both hands on the gunwales to steady the canoe. "This is a very old wood and canvas canoe," he said, "and I would hate for it to get scratched or damaged in any way. So we do it this way." To Nika, he gestured at the front seat with his head.

"My boots will get wet," she protested.

Ian looked down at his own wet boots and smiled.

"Okay," she said with exasperation. She splashed out, and as she climbed in, she scooped up a few quarts of water. The coolness of the water filled her boots. It wasn't as bad as she thought it would be.

At first the paddling was easy. They glided soundlessly over the still water. It was so different from the noisy motorboat, to really feel and hear the water moving under them. Nika was impressed that they were carrying everything they would need for three days in just three packs. This was what it must have been like a long time ago. As they turned up a long bay of Anchor Lake, Ian told them that from now on they were in a wilderness area, where cabins or motors weren't allowed, just canoes and campsites. He said people needed permits from the Forest Service to come here.

On the first portage Ian carried a pack and the canoe, whistling as he bobbed up the narrow, winding trail that connected Anchor Lake to the next small lake. Nika's pack was heavy, but when they got to the end of the portage, she felt like she'd really accomplished something. After the next portage, Randall took a turn paddling and Nika duffed as they headed down a winding river edged with tall grasses. They stopped paddling to watch a moose lift her head from the water, dripping water and weeds from her mouth. After a short muddy portage to

Elbow Lake, they paddled through a narrows, then crossed an expanse of water. Everything was so quiet, except for the splashing of their paddles and the bird song from the shore. They pulled into a tiny island to switch places and have a trail lunch. After eating, Randall seemed glad to be the duffer again, spreading a big yellow and blue map across his knees.

Nika didn't want to admit how rubbery and sore her arms were getting. The next portage was rocky, and she tripped and went over on her back like a flipped turtle, her legs waving in the air. Ian took the pack while she got to her feet, then loaded her up again. The portage ended at a beach, and she was relieved to wade in and have Ian unload her pack into the canoe. This lake was called Serpent Lake. On the map it was a long lake with lots of bays and lots of bends. Ian stopped and showed them how to use the compass. Randall held it, and as they paddled between small rock islands crowned with trees, he shouted which way was north.

"It looks like we might have already gone five miles," Randall said, studying the map.

To Nika, it felt like twenty.

"Randall, see the red dot?" Ian said. "Now see if you can locate the campsite up ahead."

Randall kept looking down at the map, then pointing excitedly as they got close. Ian aimed the canoe toward a smooth rock point that sloped down into the lake. There was no sign that anyone had ever been here before. After guiding the canoe in sideways, Ian hopped into the water to hold it as they stepped carefully across slippery rocks.

It took just a few minutes to set up the four-person yellow nylon tent with a blue rain fly. As they stood admiring their work, Ian said, "Well, Randall, shall we get ready to catch some dinner?"

Randall raced off.

Ian efficiently tucked bags and personal gear into the tent, opened the valves on the sleeping pads to let them fill, then zipped the door.

In about three minutes Randall was back, ready and waiting, decked out with pole, stringer for the fish, bait box, hat, life jacket, and a grin.

"Are you going to fish with us?" Ian asked Nika.

"Thanks, but I think I'll read for a while." After he nodded and left, she pulled open the zipper and crawled into the yellow tent, zipping it shut again.

Zeus stood with his nose pressed to the nylon screen for a bit, then she heard the jingle of his collar as he trotted off to join the fishermen down on the shore.

She closed the valve of the sleeping pad that had magically filled with air and stretched out on her bag, shifting for a good position. It was amazingly comfy. She couldn't even feel rocks poking her back. From her pack she pulled *Julie of the Wolves,* which she was reading for the third time. Ian had said that as a wolf biologist he didn't think it very probable that a wolf would regurgitate food for a human. He had also said wolf table manners were pretty rough, since they used their teeth to make decisions about who gets what. Maybe it was unlikely that wolves would share food with a human, but Nika loved the story just the same. How the wolves communicated was great, and so was how the pack members interacted. But probably the best part was how Julie loved Amaroq when she hadn't really had much love in her life before. She turned to one of her favorite parts as she relaxed and listened to Randall shout each time he caught a fish.

The pan-fried walleye and bass were the best fish she'd ever eaten. Sweet white flakes broke off at the touch of a fork. Randall went down immediately after dinner to fish off the rocks again. She and Ian washed dishes in a folding dishpan away from the shore, then dried the pots and pans by the fire.

"Want some cocoa?" he asked.

"Sure," Nika answered.

Randall was shouting to hear his echo bounce back across the lake. Nika thought the echo was cool, too. "Is there anyone else on this lake, except us?" she asked Ian, sitting down on the broad back of the rock and wrapping her arms around her knees.

"Don't think so." He seemed preoccupied. It was hard for Nika to believe they were so far from everything. For her, life on the island had been extreme, but this road-less forest was a whole new level of wilderness. Probably most of the kids she'd known had never camped like this.

"Think it's going to rain tonight?" Nika searched for words to fill the empty space between them. There were definitely some topics of conversation she wanted to avoid.

"No, I don't think so," Ian said, handing her a cup of steaming cocoa in a metal cup.

"Does the tent leak?" she asked.

"No. I'm pretty sure it's tight. I haven't used this one for a while, though." He stood and paced back and forth. "Listen, Nika, I have some things to tell you. I haven't told Randall yet. I wanted to talk to you first." He poked at the fire in the grate and added several split sticks of wood.

"Okay." She felt funny in her stomach. *Here comes a lecture,* she thought.

"Well, I got a new job when I was in St. Paul." He looked at Nika.

With surprise and relief, she walked over to lean against the trunk of a giant tree. Maybe that was what he had been talking to Pearl about.

"Anyway, I'll be the new director and head biologist for a research and education facility they've been building. It's called the Center for the Study of Northern

Animals. Right here in Red Pine. Last year they bought the property, formed a board, and began rehabbing an old brick mine building that will be the visitors' center." Ian continued, "Next week we start fencing the first animal pens. I'll be pretty busy the next few months."

As she listened to him describe it in detail, Nika couldn't help but think it sounded a bit like Bristo's, wild animals locked up, except this new center would probably have plenty of food.

Ian was so full of this new thing. It was the most she'd ever heard him talk, except about wolves. He talked about how places like this provided education, making a difference for wild lands and animals. "If people don't see them and know about them, how can they care?"

Her cocoa had cooled, and she took a few sips.

"So what about your study?" Nika asked, thinking of all those wolves wandering the woods with collars beeping out their locations.

Ian paused for a moment, pulling out dried apples and chocolate and laying the treats on a rock.

"Elinor will be taking over my old wolf research job." Offering squares of chocolate, he added, "But there is something else . . ."

Nika accepted several squares and ate them slowly. Then she picked up a stick from the ground and sat down, shredding the partially decayed stick, piece by piece.

Randall shouted from the shore, "Ian! Got another smallmouth!"

"Just a sec," Ian said to Nika. "I'll just help Randall release this one."

She waited on the log and tossed sticks into the fire. Ian came back and sat down next to her. She wished he would get to the point.

"So. Well. When I was in St. Paul, I met with Ms. Nordstrom. We worked it out so you guys could stay for the rest of the summer."

So this was the news. Not that she wanted to go back to California right away. But it would have been nice if someone had asked *her* if she wanted to stay. She was about to mention this when Ian continued.

"Anyway, since you will be staying longer, we need to talk about Khan."

She went over to get some birch bark and a log for the fire. Down on the shore, she saw the black silhouette of Randall casting against the rose-and-orange-colored brush strokes of sunset. The fire flared up.

"I understand you let him run with you on the Big Island." He gave her a steady look.

"He's not going to run off. He always . . . Well, he follows me. Except that one time."

Ian sat motionless on the log, his arms resting on his knees. He said slowly, "We've spent a lot of time and energy raising that pup, all of us."

"I just wanted him to know what it felt like to be free," she said, her voice edged with emotion.

She saw Randall turn and lower his pole.

"Forget it," she said quietly. "I'm going to bed."

Behind her she heard Ian say, "Nika . . ." but then he was silent again.

She unzipped the door so fast, it got stuck, and a squad of mosquitoes streamed in before she could get the zipper moving again. She smashed as many as she could against the walls of the tent, hoping to thin out the ranks waiting for their nightly blood donations.

As she curled into her sleeping bag, she listened to the papery sound of the nylon rain fly flapping in the breeze. She was glad she'd made a run for the tent before Ian actually said the words *never ever do that again*. Was it possible that no one had told him about the skunk? No doubt, if he knew about her trips with Thomas to see Luna, he would be even less happy with her. To say nothing of Bristo's animals.

By the time Ian and Randall came to bed later, she was asleep. In the middle of the night it rained, and a small river flowed beneath the floor of their tent, seeping into their bags. As she awoke and tried to get used to the damp sleeping bag, she couldn't help thinking that Ian had said it wouldn't rain.

For several days the young human with the silver box came alone and sat quietly while the sun moved the shadows of trees. The wolf stretched out on a large flat rock and watched, smelling food. She paced back into the forest in her loose-limbed way, returning later to a new position on the ledge. There she stayed until a cloud at the horizon sliced across the sun. As usual, after the human was gone, the wolf sniffed the area where he'd been. On these days, across the hill beyond the eagle's nest, on a tapered wedge of rock, she found food.

Chapter Fifteen

Nika thought if she stayed in the warm soggy bag much longer, her skin would wrinkle up like her fingers did when she stayed in the bath too long. Randall and Ian had already gotten up. She finally crawled out and searched the tent for something to wear that wasn't wet. After shimmying into clammy jeans that stuck to her skin and an almost-dry T-shirt, she headed back to the wonderful wooden box with a hole in it that took the place of an outhouse.

When she came back, she announced, "I have a new name for the biffy. Not the outhouse, but the outbox." Randall laughed.

Ian said, with mock seriousness, "From now on, the outbox it is."

She plunked oatmeal into her plastic bowl, adorned it with dried cranberries and brown sugar, and sat on a log beside Randall. When she looked sideways at her brother, he was smiling at her, with that irresistible grin he had. She punched him in the arm and smiled back.

Ian seemed upbeat this morning, too. Nika hoped that meant talk about Khan was history.

"After we get the dishes done and put the wet bags and clothes out to dry in the sun, I want to show you guys something." He scraped the last bite of oatmeal from his bowl and licked the spoon. Then he pulled the hot water pot from the fire and gave it a squirt of dish soap. It took just a few minutes for the three of them to get the dishes washed and upside down on rocks to dry.

Their campsite was on a sheet of granite as big as two backyards, extending from the fire grate down to the lake. Soon socks were lined up, jeans draped over bushes, and the sleeping bags laid open on rocks in the sun.

"Better than a clothesline." Ian glanced at the neat rows of wet things.

Next he pulled several aluminum pots and cups from the food pack and started up a path toward a hill flanked by a wall of trees. Over his shoulder he asked, "Ready?" Randall scampered after him. Ian didn't even wait to see if Nika would come but crashed back through the trees out of sight. When Zeus circled back to jump on her and whine, Nika decided to follow.

The path became steep past the first trees. They climbed higher and higher until they were on a ridge where they could see down the blue distance to faraway shores of the lake. She smelled that sweet herbal smell again, the one she'd smelled on the Big Island. Ian bent down, grinned, and pointed. He picked a handful for both of them to see. Blueberries. Small ones. These were like the green berries she had seen on the Big Island, except they were blue. A whole hillside of blue. Nika put one in her mouth. The taste was sharp and sweet, better than the fat puffy blueberries from the store. Ian laughed as he watched her face. The three of them went to work. For a long time there was no sound except the drumming of blueberries onto the bottoms of aluminum pots.

"Wow," said Randall, looking at an inch of blue-berries at the bottom of his pot.

"Look over here, Randall! These are big ones!" Ian exclaimed.

Nika moved to a new patch of little bushes heavy with berries, eating most of what she picked. Ian looked her way as she stuffed another handful in her mouth, as though she were unwrapping a gift he'd given her. He smiled, then returned to picking. She was blown away that the blueberries just grew here. Nobody planted them. Maybe they had been growing here for a thousand years. Or more. Eagerly she began filling her own pot.

For the next two days they stuffed themselves with blueberries, putting them in pancakes and oatmeal or just eating them by the handful. Randall's favorite was blueberries in hot pudding after dinner. Ian had brought a special hard plastic box to protect the berries in the pack, so they could bring some back to Pearl.

Even though the wolves and Thomas were never far from Nika's mind, she began to enjoy the adventure. Ian took them to explore Serpent Lake by canoe, poking into sand beaches for a swim, looking for the deepest spots off rock ledges to fish. She'd toughened up, not much minding that she had swellings and welts from various insects, or that her skin was peeling and tanned from hours in the sun. Except for the flood that first night, the weather stayed clear the whole time. They swam off the rocks at their campsite whenever they felt like it. She even caught two fish. Ian sang silly songs around the campfire and taught them the words. He showed them how to cook pancakes and noodle-mix dinners over the fire. Randall caught a northern pike almost as long as Ian's leg. Ian took at least sixty pictures before they let it go.

The last night on Serpent Lake, they built up the campfire and sat together watching the setting sun flare through folds of clouds, changing layers to peach and pink and purple. Close to them on the lake they heard the familiar haunting two-tone call hang above the surface of the darkening water. Then came the two-tone answer. It didn't matter how many times Nika heard loons—the mysterious music always thrilled her. They sounded like Native American flutes she'd heard at the farmer's market, or oboes in school orchestra. Another call came from a different direction. Soon eight or ten loons flew down one by one to land on the water. The night was so quiet, they could hear each splash as birds joined the group. The loons drifted together as the plate-size moon rose up behind the black outline of trees on the other side of the lake.

"It's almost like one of the loons called a meeting," Randall said.

"It's pretty cool to camp like this for a week or longer, to really get into the rhythm," Ian said, making two trips to bring cups, packets of cocoa, and a pot of hot water over to where they sat. "Next time we'll go for longer."

Next time? Nika thought. What did he mean? But he didn't say anything more.

Nika decided the main questions she wanted to ask couldn't wait any longer. "Well, I know we'll be going home soon. So I'll just ask. I mean, why didn't we ever know you before?" She looked at Randall. He sat up straighter and glanced at her with a worried expression.

Ian paused and then spoke. "I know I mentioned in my letter that your dad and I weren't very close. I went off to college when he was still a little boy and then to jobs overseas."

Both Randall and Nika sat very still.

"Also, I guess I was the kind of guy who loved his work so much, I let other stuff go. I saw you, Nika, as a baby, and then after getting my degree in wildlife biology I took off, going from job to job, and school to school. You probably can't understand this, but years can go by like that. It was Kate and Sean's fault, too. We all just gave up trying to communicate. I heard through friends that Randall was born and then that Sean lost his job and joined the military. Then we lost him in that munitions accident overseas."

Randall scooted closer to Nika on the rock.

"After his funeral I left calls for your mom. She never called back. Then she moved your family to California. I figured she would remarry. I ended up studying wolves in the remote forests of Finland and Russia and was completely out of touch for a few years.

"When I finally came back, I wondered about you kids. So I sent a Christmas card, and it came back. I imagined Kate had moved on and that that was what she wanted." Several moments passed. "And then that letter came from Ms. Nordstrom."

If he ran off to Russia once, what would stop him from

disappearing again? Nika wondered. Maybe there were wolves in Ethiopia or Tibet that needed studying . . .

Then Ian cleared his throat and looked at her. "I've told Randall about the job in Red Pine."

Hearing a single splash, Nika looked out at the dark water. A fish perhaps, or a frog.

"And Ian says I can help out at the Center," said Randall, tapping her arm. "We can stay all summer, Neeks. Awesome, huh?"

Two loons now started up a back-and-forth conversation farther down the lake. They sounded lonely, as if they were calling at the beginning of the world. A third loon made its wild hysterical laugh.

Ian rose to his feet and began putting food and gear away for the night. "Hey, Randall, would you—"

But before Ian got the words out, Randall grinned, grabbed a bucket, and hopped down to the lake in the thin light, as agile as a mountain goat. He spilled half the water coming back, but still had plenty to put out the fire.

It must have been three in the morning when Nika got up to go to the outbox. Zeus dutifully shook himself and joined her. In the pressing dark, the tangy damp air, and the tiptoe stillness, she was grateful for his company. Following the path back from the outbox, the narrow cone of light from her flashlight darted through the trees.

Reaching the tent, she stopped to listen to the rat-a-tat-tat of loon wings hitting the water at takeoff. Ian had told her about how they have a hard time getting airborne because they're heavy in the front, for diving, and their bones aren't hollow like other birds'. Over by the fireplace rocks, she was surprised to see the black outline of Ian, the sky behind him impossibly bright.

"Why don't you get Randall and come out here?" he asked quietly.

She stood by the tent for a minute, wanting to crawl back into her bag. Then curiosity pulled at her, and she wiggled through the tent door to shake Randall's foot. "Ian says come," she said, shaking him again. Like a sleepwalker, Randall rose, staggered outside, and fell into line behind the weaving beam of her flashlight.

When they found Ian by the fire grate, he put his hands on their shoulders and slowly guided them forward over the smooth rock toward the lake. It was funny, but she felt different now that she knew why he'd been gone from their lives. It hadn't been all his fault.

"Now look up," he said.

Nika couldn't understand what she was seeing. Randall rubbed his eyes. The sky was flowing with shivering scarves of pastel-colored light. Greens, pinks, pale yellow—there were ribbons unfolding, a swelling glimmer as the horizon pulsed and faded. There were skittering falls of light. They sat down on the still-warm rock.

"Northern lights," Ian said. "The aurora borealis."

The light oozed and shuddered, a show just for the three of them. Each time one section of the northern sky faded, another tumbled with new light shapes.

"Wow," Randall whispered.

It was like being in church, Nika thought, or an art museum. You whispered because voices would disturb the beauty.

Always the science guy, Ian explained, "It's caused by energy that streams with charged particles coming from the sun. They flow through twisted bundles of magnetic fields connecting with the upper atmosphere. Like sun storms, kind of," he said.

"Wow," Randall said again.

Nika thought Ian sounded like her science teacher last year. Silently, she watched for each new blossoming wave of light.

"But it doesn't much matter what causes them, does it? They're incredible," Ian concluded in the pin-drop quiet.

Nika hadn't wanted to come on this camping trip, but now, after the northern lights, the blueberries, the paddling on the clean water, the wing beats at sunset, her heart felt new and fresh. The sky was singing, and she loved the song. And she didn't pull away when Ian looped arms around them both and hugged them closer. She huddled into his warmth, shivering. Finally, he helped them to their feet and guided them back to the tent.

o o o

In the morning, after packing her personal things, Nika slipped away to be by herself for a few minutes. Randall was squeezing in a last bout of fishing, and Ian was beating up the pancake batter. She picked her way down the rock to a perfect flat spot and noticed again the smooth grooves carved in the rock face, like giant claw marks. She touched the grooves, then rolled back until she was flat against the cool embrace of the rock.

Yesterday, Ian had told them that the grooves in this rock had been made by glaciers ten thousand years ago. Almost eight hundred times her lifetime so far. As she lay back with her eyes closed, she wondered if there had been wolves here back then. Ian really dazzled them when he said the rock itself was 2.7 billion years old. Billion with a *B*. She felt like a moth or an otter on this ancient rock and wondered how humans had got to thinking they were so important, with their bad TV and endless malls, when this rock had been here almost since the beginning of time. Ian had been saying that wild places are important because there's no other way to know completely about how deep nature is except to lie on a rock like this, listen to water slapping the shore, watch dragonflies patrolling, and to smell deep down what the earth has always been. Now she understood.

Just then Ian called, "Breakfast! Come and get it!"

She didn't know what it was, but something felt different this morning. She climbed back up the rock and joined Ian and Randall in front of the snapping fire. Ian held out a plate of pancakes covered with maple syrup and blueberries.

She took the steaming plate, looked at Ian, and smiled. "Thanks, Uncle Ian."

For a minute he looked surprised, then he answered, "You're very welcome, Niece Nika," and handed her a camping fork.

One morning the silvery-tan wolf heard a boat pass slowly by. There was no metal sound. When the two humans came that afternoon, the light-colored wolf stayed deep in the trees. After they left, there was meat unlike anything the wolf had eaten since being with the woman. There were large slabs of the best meat, ripe wild meat with the taste of the forest. First chasing the eagles away, she ate until her belly bulged. When she couldn't eat anymore, she took scraps off to the center of the island, where she cached them for another day, using her nose to cover them with dirt and moss.

Chapter Sixteen

After making one last sweep of the campsite for forgotten items, they shoved off into a stiff wind, paddling extra hard to make progress through choppy water.

The canoe bounced on the waves, and the crosswinds made it hard to keep going straight. Randall was the duffer and sat holding tight to his tackle box. Ian was a machine as he dipped his paddle and pulled them forward. Nika hunched over as she stroked, not sure she was helping very much. But she kept paddling and soon saw their progress measured by the shore, a new point, new trees, and a small bay that suddenly came into view. Maybe she had become stronger than she thought. She dug in even harder and began to enjoy the feeling of conquering the rough water.

When they pulled into the inlet between Big Berry and Little Berry, Nika was exhausted. The hardest part in the journey home hadn't been the portages. It had been crossing the wide-open expanse of Anchor Lake against the wind and waves. In the protection of the inlet at last, they all waded while unloading, then flipped the canoe over on the sand. Fine droplets of rain and spray from the waves had soaked their things. Their clammy packs were heavier as they carried them up the hill and deposited them in the pup porch, where they could spread things out to dry. Ian shoved what remained of Khan's feeding bottles and semidestroyed blankets into a corner to make room, and started sorting through gear and left-over food.

Randall looked smaller and sad, his confidence melted for some unknown reason. He hunkered down on the old smelly sleeping bag and tucked his arms around his knees. He didn't offer to help, and they left him alone.

Nika was helping Ian string clotheslines and accidentally dropped the rope, getting it tangled. She heard Thomas's voice as he entered the porch from the kitchen, "Have you seen the shed yet?" He came over to give her a hand. Together the three of them strung line and hung soggy tents and sleeping bags. Nika felt Thomas's eyes on her the whole time.

When everything was hung, she gathered up the rest of her things to take them up to her room. Just as she took a step to leave, Thomas came up close to her and whispered, "Bonanza." She looked at him like he was out of his mind.

But Thomas kept looking at her with a funny half-smile.

Finally, her hands on her hips, she asked sharply, "What?"

"Want to go see the shed?" he said, overly cheerful and loud.

Nika wrinkled her forehead. What was going on with Thomas?

Randall left his personal things in a damp, smelly heap, went into the house, and called for Pearl. In seconds, he was back, his mood completely changed. "A bear got into the freezer, and he ate a bunch of berries and stuff and he tore the wires, so everything's wrecked! Especially the venison. He ripped a screen, and Pearl wants help with the mess when you're done. He ate a pie!" He seemed proud that he had this wonderful disaster to report.

"Yeah, I came over to help." Thomas said, "Nika, maybe you and I can haul some of the spoiled venison to town. Elinor said the Center has a freezer ready for keeping roadkill and she said we could bring some of the meat." His eyes were extra-wide open and boring into hers.

Finally, Nika understood. Suddenly excited, she asked Ian, "Can Khan have some of the venison?"

Preoccupied with saving what he could of the slightly damp leftover camping food, Ian said, "Sure, we'll hack off some pup-size bits."

In a brisk businesslike voice, Nika said to Thomas, "I've got to go see Khan for a minute, then I'll change, and we can take the venison." Randall shrank down on the sleeping bag again, as he listened to her making plans with Thomas. Once again they weren't including him.

"Want to come see Khan?" she asked her brother.

Khan greeted Nika and Randall by wagging and squirming and whimpering. Nika pushed him over on his side and rubbed his belly. He had put on a few more pounds while they were gone. There was no puppy roundness left. It seemed that in days he had become more long legged and graceful, his face lengthening, his ears taller. Randall knelt down to pet his back. Khan leaped up again and ran laps in excitement.

Elinor was sitting cross-legged on top of a picnic table in the corner of the pen, working on a pile of papers. "How was the canoe trip?" she asked with a smile. She flipped her long reddish-blond braid over her shoulder.

"Good," Nika answered as Khan charged around the pen. She put her hand up to her sunburned nose and cheeks. "I didn't quite get the sunscreen on in time. It was fun, though."

Eyes wide with stories to tell, Randall said, "Nika actually fished. I caught a whole bunch. Mostly bass. One *really* big northern!" He stretched his arms wide.

Nika had to smile at her brother. He acted like he was born for this new life of water and fish and tackle boxes and tents and sleeping bags drying in the sun.

"And there were northern lights!" he added.

When they came down, Ian was still sorting equipment in the porch.

"Lunch is almost ready," he said, nodding toward the kitchen. He took a step toward Elinor, glanced at Nika, and then stopped, blushing beneath his tan.

In the kitchen Thomas pitched in to help Pearl stack bowls and plates and silverware on a tray and carry it to the table.

"Come on everyone, let's eat," said Pearl, bringing hot blueberry muffins and a humongous bowl of chili. "We'll have to eat the food missed by our bear friend's looting before it spoils. There were a few quarts of berries that made it and some chili that was still frozen solid." She paused at the table. "It's rare for a bear to break in. I should have kept the shed door closed. He went right through the screen. I can't believe he ate frozen berries!"

"Luckily we just brought you more," said Ian. "Looks like you're going to have to update your seventies freezer, though."

Nika edged toward the door, trying to get Thomas's attention. She wanted to leave immediately for their mission.

But when he noticed, he said, "I'm hungry. Come on, Nika, let's eat."

"Okay, okay," she said.

Thomas smiled at Nika as they down next to each other and helped themselves to chili.

"Nika still runs with Khan on the Big Island, even after Khan chased the skunk," said Randall from the other end of the table, where he sat as close as possible to Ian. He smirked at his sister. In all their time as siblings, Nika had never known Randall to be a tattletale, or to be mean. She snapped her eyes to lock onto her brother's face. He stirred his chili and shrugged.

"Thanks, Randall," she said sarcastically.

Calmly buttering a muffin, Ian said, "Well, please, Nika, I'd like you to stop taking Khan out alone. We talked about this on the canoe trip. None of us wants something to happen to him, or you. The skunk thing turned out okay, but you were lucky."

"He likes it," Nika said. She wanted to say more, but the look on Ian's face stopped her.

A carrot salad was passed from hand to hand with no words spoken.

Elinor finally broke the silence. "Those new pens are really coming along." She smiled and scooped out some salad.

"I'm anxious to see the progress," Ian added, nodding.

Nika kept noticing how Ian shot quick looks at Elinor during lunch, like they had a secret. Nika didn't know why it bothered her. She should be glad Ian could finally unbolt his attention from his work long enough to notice something besides radio collars and statistics and blueprints for renovations.

"What pens?" Randall asked in a food-muffled voice, filling his face with a muffin he held with both hands.

Ian let out a long breath and cast an uncertain look at Elinor.

"What pens?" asked Nika, looking back and forth from one adult to the other.

"For the first resident animals at the Center," Elinor answered brightly, getting up from the table. "Anyone want more water or milk?"

Pearl leaned back in her chair with her eyebrows raised in expectation.

Ian looked around for a minute, then said, "Well, this wasn't the way I planned to talk about this."

All of them looked at him and waited.

Thomas looked uncomfortable and started quietly battling his fork with his spoon.

"We're hoping that Khan will be our first resident. Things are coming along so well with his socialization." He looked straight ahead. It was hard to know whom he was looking at.

Nika stood. Of course. Had she really thought that raising this wolf pup meant she had some say about what happened to him? No one had even discussed it with her. Would that have been too much to ask?

"He should be free to run. Like on the Big Island!" She threw down her napkin and shoved her heavy wooden chair away from the table. "Not live his life in a cage."

"It just can't be that way—you know that. Besides, a couple of acres is not a cage," Ian answered in a level, no-fooling-around kind of voice. "I'm sorry."

Had he always known what he was going to do with Khan but just waited until the last minute to tell? She felt a bloom of dark anger.

"Sorry for what? Sorry for everything? Me, too. I'm sorry we came here." Nika hurtled out the back door, allowing the screen to bang shut, and ran up the hill to Khan's pen. She heard footsteps behind her and looked back to see Thomas following.

The pup looked startled as she clanged through the gate. Nika had learned that wolves can be very sensitive to loud noises and emotional upsets. She slowed herself, opened the gate quietly for Thomas, and went down on her knees. Khan approached slowly at first, then fell on her with licks and nibbles at her chin. Thomas squatted down and got licks as well.

"I brought my camera. I'll be your paparazzi," he said. "After all, you should have photos of you and Khan in the woods, in case you ever write a book about him or something."

"Let's go," she said. She opened the gate, and they all raced down the path to the Big Island, Khan almost tangled in their legs.

She slowed at the sand spit so Khan could take a long drink. Thomas snapped a picture. As the three of them ran the familiar path toward the rendezvous site, Nika wondered how things could seem so bad when just yesterday they had seemed so good.

When she came back from running Khan with Thomas, Nika discovered that Ian and Elinor and Randall had unexpectedly left. And Pearl was up working in her garden. Nika had been so upset, but now she wondered if they'd left her behind on purpose.

Thomas called her from the front of the cabin. "Nika, are you coming?"

"Can you believe it?" Thomas asked as they hauled the last load of spoiled venison down to the dock. The small boat rode a little lower in the water from the load.

He steered out into gray water and gray skies. As they rounded the point and headed across Anchor Lake, the wind picked up. With the wind and the motor noise, it was hard to hear each other talk. "We'll talk when we get into the lee of Eagle Island," Thomas shouted, "with our bonanza!" Now that they were off by themselves, Nika couldn't stop smiling. Wouldn't Luna be surprised!

Finally in the shelter of the small island, they turned off the motor and coasted to shore. Nika asked, "So what are we going to do? It's a lot of meat for one wolf!"

"I've been thinking about it. We have to take some to Elinor. I figure that if Luna was wild and she found a whole roadkilled deer carcass, she would work on it over a long period of time and probably bury a bunch for later. They're not as picky about expiration dates as we are." The boat thunked and scraped up onto the skid logs. "I think we should give her at least half, don't you?"

"Sure, and then we can come back and just watch and not worry about food for a while."

They unloaded deer meat wrapped in white paper packages and hauled it up the hill, making several trips. When all the meat had been plopped in a bloody heap on some moss behind a large boulder, they took the paper and went back down to their watching spot. Near the shore Thomas made a ring of rocks and piled up some dry twigs. He put the wadded paper in the ring and took some matches from his pocket. The damp paper burned slowly, and he had to keep adding twigs to keep it going.

They waited for an hour, expecting the wolf to leap upon the pile of meat and devour it, but there was no sign of Luna. Finally, they decided they'd better take the rest of the meat to Elinor.

"Let's come back tomorrow," said Nika.

"I heard about a storm warning for tomorrow," answered Thomas, seeming to calculate in his head.

"Well, we could come early."

"Should be okay, I don't think it's supposed to really storm until later." Thomas doused the remains of the fire before they launched the boat.

In town the two of them loaded the remaining wrapped meat into an old wagon that Thomas kept stashed by the main docks, pulling together to haul it up the hill.

As they approached the Center, Nika thought it didn't exactly look finished. The main brick building had carpenter's tools and piles of materials lying about. New observation windows across one side still had brand stickers glued to them. Elinor was inside, busy at her computer. She directed them to the new walk-in freezer out the back door and went back to work, leaving them to unload. The packages of meat looked pretty puny in a freezer that must have been designed for a whole herd of road-killed deer hanging from hooks. It was good Elinor hadn't come with them. She might have wondered why they hadn't brought more.

On the way back to the island, Nika thought out different scenarios for the two wolves. Scenario one: Put them both on Eagle Island and bring them food. Problem: The ice freezes in the winter and the wolves might leave to hunt. If they went toward town, someone might shoot them for coming close to farms or houses. Ian said that happened. She kept reading that captive wolves in the wild would most likely starve from undeveloped hunting skills and no pack to hunt with. They could die from being shot, or if they invaded the territory of a pack of wild wolves, they could be killed.

Scenario two: Release them where they first found Khan. They could have pups and become a pack far away from people. Problem: How would Thomas and Nika catch Luna by themselves to move her? Khan had never been in a boat. Would he get desperate and hurt himself? And again, could they learn to hunt on their own?

Scenario three: They could find an adult to help them release the two wolves. Problem: There wasn't an adult who would agree to what they wanted to do. Scenario four: Take Khan back to California and find a wildlife sanctuary where she could visit him. Problem: Wouldn't it mess him up to be caged, drugged, and put on a plane and wake up in a whole new place? Besides, if she hated the thought of him locked up here, why would California be any different?

Scenario five: Talk Ian into adopting all of them, Randall, Nika, Luna, and Khan, and buying a big piece of land right at the edge of the roadless wilderness where the wolves could come and go. Thomas told her about a couple of naturalists who lived near Red Pine who watched a pack of wolves that lived near them for years. The people hid in blinds and observed and took pictures with long lenses. Problem: For her, that would mean making a home here, not that she had been invited. The land would have to be far away from farms and towns, with a national forest or something nearby. And would Ian do it anyway? He had his heart set on this educational center and his star wolf, little orphan Khan. And, besides, was he really the type to settle down and raise a couple of kids who weren't even his own?

Unfortunately, from all the reading she had done, she now knew keeping a wolf isn't simple. And there were permits and laws. Legally, Khan belonged to the state.

By the time they motored back to Pearl's dock, Nika had a headache from thinking. Maybe she could sleep on it, and a solution would become clear.

"At seven tomorrow," Thomas said as he pushed off to head for home. "No later, or we might have to worry about the storm."

When she got home, Ian was still gone. She had a quiet supper with Pearl and wondered where Ian was. She had thought he would be waiting to talk to her. After all, she had said she was sorry they had ever come and then had run out. Maybe the fact that he was gone meant he'd given up, and there was nothing to say.

She went to bed early but couldn't sleep. The wind tossed the trees and whistled in the eaves, and she felt disconnected and alone. Finally she slept but jerked awake with a whole dream clear in her mind like a movie. She had been sitting on the floor in the corner of a huge high-ceilinged room. Everyone in the large crowd was standing around taking turns talking. Then the mood changed and everyone hugged. She couldn't make out their words, but she thought, *They don't need me here. I have nothing to say.* Then a large black wolf entered a door on the far side of the room. Some people were afraid and backed away. The wolf began to weave calmly through the crowd, his eyes and ears alert as he walked. He was coming straight toward her. After he arrived beside her, he turned and faced the crowd, standing as still as stone. Everyone turned to look. Slowly she reached out one hand and laid it on the wolf's back. His fur was inches deep and closed around her wrist. She rose to her feet, steadying herself with one hand on his back. When she was standing, she realized how big he was, his back at waist height. People smiled and asked questions. Suddenly she understood that she was expected to speak. Her voice felt clear and strong. People listened. She knew the wolf had come just for her. The wolf leaned closer, his shoulder pressing against her, and she once again sank her hand into the fur over his shoulders, feeling changed somehow.

As she lay in the darkness, she tried to remember the words she'd spoken to the crowd, but the dream folded shut and drifted away like a loose kite.

The wolf sensed a change in the air. The young humans came late in the day and sat very still. In spite of her fear, the silvery-tan wolf was drawn to them. The one-like-the-woman puppy-whined. Hesitating at first and alert to far-away thunder, the wolf advanced on bent legs. Halfway down from the protection of trees, she urinated, then inched forward until she was several body lengths away. She lifted her lips in a smile and lowered her head and body in greeting.

Chapter Seventeen

Thomas would be by to pick her up at seven a.m., so she'd better hurry. Now that Randall had made the subject so public, she shouldn't be taking Khan for runs at all. But, it probably didn't matter. Khan would soon be living the rest of his life as a media attraction. For her, it was worth risking Ian's anger to give Khan at least one more taste of freedom.

Nika got up, dressed in jeans and a sweatshirt, grabbed her rain poncho and anorak, and tiptoed into the morning. After lacing on her leather boots, she headed up to see Khan. Rose light spilled into the treetops. Lengths of chiffon mist wound through the tree trunks as she hurried up to the pen. The ground was dry, even though the sky still looked overcast. On the canoe trip Ian had said something about how dry ground in the morning meant it was going to rain, or it wasn't. She couldn't remember.

Khan leaped at the fence when she arrived. He was eleven and a half weeks old now and weighed thirty-two pounds, with large paws and long limbs like a perfect little wolf. His ears were too big for his head and were in a constant commotion of alertness and intensity. His eyes had almost completely changed from blue to amber. Ian left parts of deer legs for him to eat in his pen overnight, but he still loved chicken the best. He enjoyed cooling off in his pool, especially when they brought chunks of ice for him to play with. He had been a well-mannered wolf for his puppy checkup and shots with Dr. Dave. His workouts with Maki's big lab Trucker had been good for him, giving him the experience of being dominated and playing wild chase.

Nika pressed his vitamin meatballs against the wire, and while he devoured them, she slipped through the gate and hunkered down. He licked and leaped, trying always to reach her mouth and lips, whimpering the whole time. When he turned to race around the pen, she placed a chunk of hand-me-down venison on top of his favorite rock. He found it, grabbed it, then circled the pen. He stopped to eat a few bites, but soon ran with it again. He'd grown so fast!

But as she opened the gate, for a minute she felt almost unable to breathe. What if she did lose the pup? Her whole world would turn upside-down. Again. Suddenly a black streak flew past her and straight down the path toward the sand spit. At the beach Khan doubled back to check on her. She trotted behind him up the path on the Big Island, surprised when he peeked out from behind a tree. They played this game all the way to the beach overlook. When they arrived at the rendezvous site, Khan sniffed every inch of the small clearing. Nika sat down on the dry ground.

Thomas had been right about the weather—the sky looked like it had sponged up water and was holding it in heavy gray layers. Khan soon flopped beside her and turned over for his deserved belly rub. The pup pressed his oversize feet against her leg. She separated the pads with her fingers, as she'd done since he was tiny, massaging them. She was always intrigued by the skin webs between the toes. Elinor had given her a little lecture on wolf body parts, and one thing she'd said was that their big feet were almost like snowshoes in winter and that they helped them travel over uneven ground. Nika closed her eyes as she held the pup's paw in hers. For a while, neither of them moved.

When she heard the buzz of an outboard motor, she jumped up. It must be Thomas. She pulled out the deer tail she'd brought today and dangled it. Khan followed more slowly going back, like a kid being called in from recess, sniffing along the way and squatting to mark every few feet with tiny shots of urine. Finally she slapped the deer tail against her leg and ran. With lolling tongue, Khan swept by her and down the hill, vanishing in the dense green on the other side of the sand spit. He would beat her home.

Feeling exhilarated from their run, she jogged the last few yards to the pen. But Khan was nowhere to be seen, and the pen gate was closed. When her hand reached for the latch, she saw Ian kneeling down on the far side, where the big pines grew. She had been so sure he'd been asleep when they left. Khan was licking Ian's face and lips. Ian rose, put one hand on his neck, and looked at her. Khan raced toward the gate, then back to Ian.

Quickly and without thinking, Nika grabbed her rain poncho from where she'd hung it on a bush, and hurried down the trail. She heard Ian call her name. Just as she reached Pearl's cabin, she heard the gate clang and rapid footsteps down the path. She felt panic rising. Her stomach tightened, making it hard to breathe. She slowed, then stopped and brought her hands to her hips.

"Did you hear me call?" Ian asked.

Nika turned to face him. "Thomas is waiting at the dock. I've got to go."

Ian looked away and said, "Later. You can go with Thomas later. Right now you are going to the Center with me. I want you to see the enclosure we built for Khan. You can help out for a while."

She felt confused. Wasn't he going to say something about yesterday or about her morning run with Khan? But he didn't seem angry. Just unwavering.

"Okay." She hated this. The enclosure they built for Khan. "Can Thomas come?"

"Have him come to town later. If the weather holds, you can go with him for a while before supper," Ian answered, pulling open the kitchen door.

All day in town! Nika opened her mouth to protest, but Ian stopped her. "Go and tell Thomas. I'll meet you at the big boat."

It was a long day. Ian came up with project after project for Nika. First he had her sorting greeting cards of different northern animals and putting them in plastic sleeves for the gift shop. He asked her to mop the office floor that was already so clean, she could hardly see where her mop had been. She unpacked and sorted brochures Elinor had ordered. Nika simmered with impatience, refusing the chicken and avocado sandwich Ian offered her.

In the afternoon, Ian and Elinor showed her the fenced area, roughly the size of two football fields, much larger than she had imagined. They talked about it proudly. It had trees, a small concrete pond with a waterfall, and big rocks all around. Elinor kept going on and on about the den they were having workmen dig. But as Nika looked over the neatly landscaped pen where Khan would live, she could only think how lonely he would be, how he would spend all day standing at the fence.

Finally Ian said, "Okay, off you go. But I want you to help out again tomorrow."

Thomas's boat drifted and thumped against the town dock. Hopping in, Nika pushed off, saying, "Let's go!"

Thomas backed the boat, then shifted into forward gear. "We can probably still beat the storm," he shouted over the motor.

Nika looked up. It wasn't raining at all, even though the sky looked like gray hammocks full of water. It was odd that the wind was blowing toward the storm, she thought. Maybe it was going away.

Thomas pulled the boat up on the skid logs and tied up to a tree. They didn't need to remind each other to be very quiet as they walked to their usual observation spot, next to the chair-shaped tree trunk. Thomas opened his backpack, took out his camera, and handed binoculars to Nika.

At first it looked like all the meat they'd left was gone. Nika saw one raggedy chunk partially covered with dirt. Both of them looked for Luna. There was no sign of her. Then they saw an ear flick. She was stretched out in shadows just inside the margin of the forest. Her golden eyes were turned their way. Finally she raised her head and shoulders and shifted to face them, but she didn't stand up.

It seemed like hours passed as they sat watching the wolf watch them. The sky continued to darken, but they agreed the storm was still far away. When Luna stood and stretched, they thought she would go to the cache and eat, but she didn't. She stood tall on her long thin legs, looking down at them. Then slowly, but with a bounce in her step, she trotted directly toward them. Nika and Thomas sat up straight. Nika took a breath and waited. Thomas snapped several pictures, then put his camera away. They looked at each other, not believing what was happening. Thomas whispered, "Look away." Nika nodded.

They averted their eyes so they wouldn't scare her. They heard her feet crunch lichen and sticks nearby. Nika looked up and pup-whined and whimpered and said, "Hey Luna-girl, hey girl." Luna edged toward them pausing and ducking and finally threw herself down on a mat of moss growing in a hollow not far away. Nika continued to croon. The wolf wagged the tip of her tail, making a low groaning sound, and lay still, moving nothing but her eyes. It seemed forever that they sat like that. Nika badly wanted to get close enough to touch her, but Thomas wasn't so sure it was a good idea. They decided it was best to be patient, as she'd learned to be with Khan.

"This is magical," Nika said when she stopped holding her breath at last.

"Yeah, and she's telling us something, too, something important," whispered Thomas. Nika looked at him and waited.

"I think she just told us that she really was raised by humans. I'll bet that once she felt safe with some person. Not Bristo. Maybe a woman, because she seemed to respond when you called." Nika nodded. It was true. From what she'd read recently, no wild wolf would ever act as Luna was acting now.

A rumble of thunder rolled down the lake. The southwestern sky looked bruised. On the horizon, dark clouds bloomed with tall white cauliflower tops. Smaller gray popcorn clouds marched in rows in front of them.

Luna was suddenly nervous. She stood, crouched, and looked around, her muscles tensed, legs bent.

"Maybe the storm is making her nervous," Nika said.

"We'd better go." Thomas slowly rose to his feet. The second they moved, the wolf glided as smoothly as moving light back up the hill, up and into the cover of dark trees.

The wolf heard sounds. She smelled smells. The smells put fire into her muscles and pulled her toward the cover of trees. She recognized the voice beneath the eagle tree. With it was the metal sound that came with humans. And beyond that, thunder, but more than thunder, fear.

Later, pain burned into the wolf's body, and she slipped back away from her body. She could smell the one-like-the-woman beside her as the wolf fell deep into the forest of her mind.

Chapter Eighteen

Before they took another step, Nika heard the unmistakable *bong* of an aluminum boat hitting rock. Thomas reached out his hand for her to be still, and the two of them inched up the shore toward the sound.

They slipped into the bushes behind the eagle tree and carefully parted dense branches to peek through. Bristo was swearing and muttering as he clumsily tugged his boat over a piece of driftwood. He fumbled and leaned forward, pulling a rifle from the seat.

Electric fear shot through Nika's body. She scrambled back across the ledge and ran, her feet tangling and tripping in knots of weeds and brush, propelled by her own racing blood. Thomas was right behind her.

At the small clearing by the chair tree, they looked up the hill, frantic to see Luna. In patchwork shadows, she was peering from several feet beyond the edge of the woods, her light face barely visible. She turned her head and looked toward the eagle tree. Her ears were air-planed to the side, uncertain, her body motionless.

What could they do? They'd heard Bristo say he would kill the runaway wolf if he could find her. Had he followed them?

"If we can get the wolf to come to us, Bristo wouldn't dare shoot," said Thomas.

"Come on, Luna," Nika called, kneeling and pup-whining, trying to keep the urgency from her voice so she wouldn't scare the wolf. She puppy-whined again. When Luna didn't come toward them, Thomas dug into his pack and produced a piece of jerky, holding it out. One of Luna's ears stood taller, the other still pulled partway back in fear. She began to move toward Nika and Thomas in a crouch, shooting glances toward the clunking noises from Bristo's boat. She circled around behind them and flattened herself in the cover of bushy junipers. Thomas tossed her a chunk of the jerky. She took it in her mouth, then dropped it.

Nika crooned, "Good girl, Luna, good girl. You can do it. Stay with us. Come on, Luna."

Nika and Thomas both realized at the same moment that there was no going home now. The sky was burly with purple clouds, and they could hear the collisions of thunder coming closer.

Thomas tried to lure Luna with another small piece of jerky. Like Hansel and Gretel and Little Red Riding Hood all mixed up, this time they were dropping crumbs for the wolf.

Luna moved closer to them, but kept her eyes and ears trained on the muffled scraping behind the eagle tree. She growled, raised her hackles, trotted in a circle, then froze and sank into the junipers again.

Nika heard a thud and saw the bushes shake beneath the eagle tree. Luna heard it too and tensed. She crouched. Then Nika and Thomas heard Bristo moving through the trees and swearing. The wolf ran up the rock heading for safety, but Bristo had cut uphill and was coming out near the feeding spot. Luna froze. Nika and Thomas saw Bristo at the edge of the trees, staring at the crouched wolf. He laughed, then raised his rifle. There was a snapping sound, like a large branch breaking in the wind, followed by a yelp of pain.

Nika yelled and ran across the rock toward the man. She didn't think and didn't care.

Thomas shouted, "Nika, don't!"

But Nika was screaming at Bristo, "Stop! Stop! I'll get my uncle. You'll go to jail!"

Halfway across the rock ledge, she tripped, her foot jammed between two rocks. Pain spiked up through her ankle. Panic dulled the pain, and she hobbled on. She couldn't see Luna. When she came around a giant boulder, she saw Bristo staggering toward the wolf with his rifle pointed down. He stopped to maintain his balance, one hand on a stump. Luna was on the ground past the boulder, at the edge of some small trees. She was bleeding from a wound in her shoulder, her head partly raised. Bristo was cursing and swaying.

Nika ran to Luna and fell to her knees beside her, screaming at Bristo, "This is what you wanted! Get out of here! You going to shoot kids, too?"

"You didn't see nuthin!" shouted Bristo, breathing heavily. "I bet you're the one let go the others so I got nuthin'. Stupid bleedin'-heart kids . . ." Bristo turned and walked haltingly away. At that moment, the wind died, and the lake went completely still.

After a snarl of engine noise and swearing, Nika heard the boat putter away from the island.

Luna wasn't moving much, but she panted and made low-pitched puppy-whines. Nika felt a sharp wave of pain from her own ankle. She slumped down next to the beautiful tan wolf. Across the lake yellow wires of light cut through the navy blue sky, followed by a grumble of thunder. Inside, Nika felt her courage collapse. Luna could die. Maybe Bristo had found her because of them. She jabbed at her tears with the back of her hand. Then taking a breath, she yelled, "Thomas!

Thomas came scrambling up with his backpack, his face frozen in fear, his mouth gaping as he stared at the downed wolf. "I thought he shot you!"

He quickly seemed to collect himself. "We'll get the vet. Touch her. Go slowly," he said.

Nika reached out and carefully lowered her hand onto the thick fur on the wolf's shoulder. Her hand came away bloody. Luna lifted her nose, then let her head drop back down again.

"Good. Now see if you can find the wound, and press, to stop the bleeding." Nika found a wet hole in Luna's bloody shoulder and pinched it together with her fingers. The wolf moaned and jerked, then looked away, as though she'd given up.

The wolf's breathing seemed to steady, and Nika started to breathe with her, feeling a strange calm. She thought about Ian, how much she needed him right now.

The wind was picking up. Thomas looked at the sky again. "The storm's gonna hit. I can just make it to town. You stay here. You're going to get pretty wet. Wait a sec. Hang on." Thomas flew down to his boat and came back with a life jacket and a boat cushion. "For insulation from the ground," he said. Then he attacked some nearby trees with the knife he always carried. He came back with armloads of branches that he began to teepee around and over her and the wolf.

As the balsam branches began to surround her, Nika

was grateful that Luna had fallen next to a dense stand of trees on brushy ground. She remembered hearing you didn't want to be next to a tall tree or on a big rock in a lightning storm.

Thomas poked his head into the ragged shelter he'd thrown up around them. "When the lightning starts, if your hair stands on end, squat on the life jacket with your head between your knees." She heard the scraping of his boots as he scrambled down to his boat. At least it was still light out. The engine started right away, and she heard his small boat move out into the lake, thumping as it bucked the waves. She was glad it wasn't far to Red Pine.

The rain fell softly at first, then increased to a rhythm of heavy drops plunked against the rocks and leaves. In the distance she could barely hear the drone of Thomas's boat. Adjusting the branches, Nika laid the life jacket and cushion so she could circle her body around Luna. As rain trickled down her face, she positioned her arm over the wolf, pressing the wound. Soon she was soaked through, shivering, and her ankle throbbed with pain. Thunder tumbled, dark sounds ripped by stabs of lightning. The storm lowered around them like a sudden fall of early night.

Nika wondered what time it had been when Thomas left. She wished she'd worn a watch. She tried to remember when Ian said he was going home today. Had he already left town? If so, who would Thomas find to help?

Spikes of lightning, explosions of thunder, wind pushing trees in dizzy circles, and slanting sheets of water all surrounded Nika and the unconscious wolf. She tried to think of something else beside her fear and the pulsing pain in her ankle. Something besides how Luna might die because of them. She thought of her old dog-friend Rookie and his knowing brown eyes. Once she had been with her mom in the mountains in a cabin, and both she and Randall had been afraid of the thunder and lightning. Her mom had made up a story about the Thunder Princess, how she had big feet, and how she made thunder when her enormous boots pounded across the sky. Nika imagined her mom cuddled up next to her now, telling the story.

Time seemed to crawl on its belly. Nika couldn't stop worrying. She had to do something to pass the eternity until someone came. She tried reciting nursery rhymes, starting with "There was an old woman tossed up in a basket," but she couldn't remember all of the words. Then she tried to remember her lines from the school play last year. She said the alphabet with an animal for each letter. Aardvark was her favorite. She bogged down with *N* and ended up singing Girl Scout songs. Finally she just sat in the dark, clutching the green jade of the necklace Olivia had made.

When the heavy rain began to let up, Nika could see the lake again. Sunset threw fingers of yellow light in fans above the leftover hunching thunderclouds. It had been a hot day before the storm, but now the temperature had dropped. She worried about Luna being cold. She remembered that when a person was injured, you were supposed to keep him warm. The wolf was unresponsive, but Nika could feel a pulse. Shivering, she put as much of her body as she could next to the wolf for warmth. At least she could feel the soft rise and fall of the wolf's breathing under her hand. "Good girl, Luna. Good girl," she said.

Nika remembered all the lonely waiting she'd experienced in her life, wondering what would happen next. And here she was waiting again, cold and soaking wet. After the sun went down, she couldn't even see beyond her foot in the storm-swept moonless night. What if Thomas's boat had broken down? If so, the only person who knew she was here was Bristo.

Finally she heard outboard motors, then a man's voice, and aluminum clonks from the landing. Soon thin bars of light were breaking and zigzagging through the trees. She shivered even more. Even her jaw was shaking. What if it was Bristo? Finally she heard low voices and one higher one. Bristo would have been alone.

"They're up the hill a little, over here." It was Thomas! In a moment shafts of light from four flashlights pinned the balsam tent. She heard the squishing of wet boots, then Thomas, Ian, Maki, and Elinor all emerged. As Thomas removed the branches, no one spoke. Maki propped a large flashlight in the crotch of a tree to light the scene.

"We got a little wet" was all Nika managed to say through chattering teeth. The three adults in their rain slickers looked down at the sodden pair. Elinor and Maki gently squatted by the wolf. Ian stood holding his flashlight, shaking his head, then went down on his knees next to Nika.

"Are you okay?" he asked.

"My ankle," she answered in a shaky voice. Now that they were here, she felt warm tears on her cold cheeks, and her nose was running.

Ian gently flexed and probed at her ankle, saying, "Does this hurt? How about this?" His voice was steady, as it had been when he'd examined the dead wolf earlier in the summer—very professional. "Well, I don't think it's broken. But we need to get you home." Then he turned to Luna and, with the same calm, quickly assessed the wound in her shoulder. The wolf seemed to be barely breathing.

"I somehow can't believe what I'm seeing." He stood and looked off toward the boats. "Thomas explained he thought this wolf came from Bristo. And you two tried to stop him?" He shook his head, wiping his face with his sleeve. She wished she could see his expression. She couldn't tell if he was proud of her, scared, or mad.

"Before he shot her, she came to us," Nika declared, trying to sound bright and brave, even though she wasn't sure she was strong enough to even stand. "She's just got to be okay . . ." Thomas stood behind Ian. Nika tried to force her shivering lips into a smile of gratitude.

Ian spoke to Elinor and Maki. "We've got to hurry. Nika is pretty cold. And the wolf . . ."

Ian helped Nika stand on one leg, then swept her up to his shoulder. "This okay?" he asked. "Hold on. It's called a fireman's carry."

Upside down, Nika craned her neck to see Elinor and Maki and Thomas lift Luna onto some kind of canvas sling. Luna didn't move. Nika took this as a bad sign. Struggling to stay on their feet and making a bizarre parade, flashlights slicing through the darkness, they carried the full-grown wolf across the wet rocks to where the boats were tied.

After Maki and Elinor loaded their canvas burden into Maki's boat, Thomas hopped in and sat by Luna, his hand keeping pressure on the wound.

"Go ahead and take the wolf to Dave!" Ian shouted.

Maki nodded. He and Elinor pushed off and climbed in. The motor started, then accelerated to an urgent-sounding high-pitched hum as they headed toward town.

Ian helped Nika across the rocks to his larger boat.

Drops of water fell from the soaked trees and waves sloshed against the shore. To keep her balance, Nika held tight to the gunwales of the big boat until Ian came to lift her over the side. She hopped up to the chair next to his in the front. Wading, Ian maneuvered the boat past the rocks, jumped over the side, started the big engine, turned on the running lights, and set out into uneasy water.

Nika couldn't believe he knew where he was going in the dark. To her it felt like being inside a windy tunnel, but when she saw the lights of Red Pine, she realized they'd rounded the far end of Eagle Island. The lights faded as they headed out into the murky lake. She felt lost as they tossed across the waves created by the storm. The powerful boat pounded the water, jarring her teeth. Her ankle shouted out with pain each time the boat hit the bottom of a trough. It wasn't long before she saw the familiar pattern of lights in Ian's cabin by the beach. They were home.

The tan wolf woke in another cage, and there was pain in her shoulder. She fell in and out of fitful sleep. The cage was small, and there was no place to hide. A man moved slowly, talked calmly, and put something smelly on her wound.

Chapter Nineteen

Pearl helped Nika out of her dripping-wet clothes and wrapped her in a white terrycloth robe big enough for two people. Bending over the lower bunk, the one Randall usually slept in, Pearl pulled back the covers and said, "Get in and get warm." She placed a pillow under Nika's foot. "Ian's trained as an EMT, you know. He knows just what to do."

Going downstairs, Pearl came back up with hot tea, chicken noodle soup, and ibuprofen, then quietly left again. After Nika finished her soup, Ian appeared with an ice pack and Ace bandages.

There was a charged silence between them as he examined her ankle. Was he going to make her be the first one to talk? When he first applied the ice, it burned, and Nika bit her lip to keep from complaining. Ian carefully wrapped the stretchy fabric and secured it.

"I'm guessing it's a bad sprain. The ibuprofen should help, but keep the foot elevated, okay? You'll have to stay off it until we can get in for an xray tomorrow." He stood quickly, gathered the first aid materials, and stuffed them back into a canvas bag. With a smile, he headed for the doorway.

"Nika? Sweetheart. Nika? How about some breakfast?"

Nika swam up through the layers of a dream until she surfaced in the bright morning light and anchored her eyes on the smiling face of Pearl. In her dream there'd been a storm. A sudden spasm of pain in her ankle reminded her, it wasn't just a dream.

"Cottage cheese blueberry pancakes this morning. And it's a beautiful day." Pearl, still smiling, propped a crutch against the bunk bed, then left.

After struggling into her shorts and a T-shirt, Nika hobbled down the steps, the crutch in one hand, holding tight to the log banister. She eased off the bottom step. Ian, Maki, and Elinor were in the living room standing in a row. She felt their eyes on her as she crutched through and out the back door in the direction of the outhouse.

When she came back, Pearl and Maki brought plates of pancakes and bacon. They all sat down. Nika noticed that Ian's clothes looked more rumpled than usual.

Elevating her foot on a second chair, Nika wondered why everyone was so quiet. Not looking at anyone, she asked, "Is Luna okay?"

"We think she's going to be," Ian said. "Dave said it was a miracle that the bullet didn't kill her. Bristo's aim was off. Lots of blood loss."

Nika wanted to jump up and run all of the way over to the Camerons' to tell Thomas. Luna was okay! They had saved her!

Ian lifted his coffee cup, then put it down again without drinking. "What if his aim had been off just a little bit more?"

Nika felt a chill shoot through her body. It was hard to imagine now that she had faced Bristo with a gun.

For a few minutes no one talked. Forks clinked on plates, and food was passed.

Then Ian cleared his throat. "What you did was extremely dangerous," he said. His voice was low. His eyes were red, as if he hadn't slept.

"You could have been badly hurt, Nika, by Bristo, or by the wolf." He pressed his lips together into a firm line.

"I'm confused about all of this," he continued. "For one

thing, I can't help but wonder how you two knew where the wolf came from." Nika glanced up to meet Ian's penetrating look. "And why you didn't tell me," he added. He seemed uncomfortable.

"Thomas saw her on the island. She had a collar. We knew a wolf had escaped from Bristo's." She looked down at her empty plate.

Placing his hands flat on the table, Ian said, "Okay, we'll get back to that. So. I know it is highly unlikely anything like this will happen again, but I think it is important to have a rule for the future. The rule is, never, ever feed a wolf! You never want a wolf to associate people with food. Period."

"We feed Khan," Nika said.

"The truth is, from the moment we took him from the den, Khan was no longer wild. A wild wolf that has been fed by people is in danger. I know of a guy who gave sandwiches to a wolf at his mailbox. The wolf didn't hurt anyone, but it lost its fear. That could have been what happened to one of our collared wolves that was shot last fall—his cut collar thrown into the lake." Ian waved his fork in his hand as he made his points.

"Also, if any wild animal associates people with food and loses his natural fear, he can be dangerous. Healthy wolves are not known to attack people, but if they are starved and feel no fear, they can decide to be aggressive to get food. They might grab a pet. When they lose fear around people because they've been fed, they're called habituated. These wolves often end up dead."

Being lectured like this made Nika feel dumb. They never would have fed a truly wild wolf. She and Thomas had been trying to help Luna, because she'd escaped from Bristo.

"Thomas made sure Luna didn't see him put down the food," she said. "We didn't want her to starve." Her voice faded. They'd saved Luna's life and everyone thought she and Thomas had made a big mistake.

"The reason she might have starved is that she's always been fed and she's never learned to hunt. Let me repeat. Never, ever feed a wild wolf, Nika. That's the rule. The more you learn about wolves, the better you will understand this." Ian looked hard into her eyes.

"Okay." She looked down and twisted her napkin into a knot. Her face was burning.

Ian heaved a huge sigh.

"Nika," said Elinor, touching her arm, "I agree with what Ian said. The best thing is to keep a lot of distance between yourself and wild animals and just appreciate their wildness."

Nika looked up to see the warmth in Elinor's gaze. "Thomas saved me," she said. "And Luna." What would Nika have done without Thomas?

"He made some good decisions. He was very brave," said Elinor.

Elinor glanced at Ian, then reached a hand toward Nika again. "Even as skinny as she is, she's a big female. If she makes it and eats well, she should near a hundred pounds."

If she makes it.

For a few minutes the room was quiet. Maki stood up and walked with his coffee cup into the kitchen. There was the sound of pouring and a clink.

Elinor forked some pancakes and bacon onto Nika's plate. "And if Luna survives, Bristo won't get her back. If we can, we'd like to find her previous owner. Maybe they let her go, or she escaped. No one knows."

So after all of that, Luna could just go back to the same stupid person who'd let her go? Nika looked away, and suddenly her ankle began to throb.

Dr. Dave kept careful watch on Luna at the clinic, treating her wound, vaccinating her, and testing her for diseases. Each day Nika listened to the community messages on the radio to find out how she was. *"And now for all of you out on those faraway isles, here are the messages for this lovely summer day . . ."* The announcer went on and on, telling about how Jed should bring the chain saw with him when he came back to town, and how Melanie missed her bus in Minneapolis, so they shouldn't send someone from Sugarloaf Island to pick her up until tomorrow.

And finally, what she was waiting for. *"Dr. Dave from the Red Pine vet's office sends Nika and Thomas a message.*

'Thumbs-up for Luna. Looking better every day.'" Not much news, but she was alive. And no matter what Ian said, Nika knew that without her and Thomas, Luna would be dead.

For Nika, after the xray confirmed her ankle wasn't broken, the invalid routine got old in one afternoon. Three days looked like a long time. Ian brought the mail, with letters from Zack and Olivia. Zack wrote her from his marine biology camp. He was learning about whales. Olivia's dance group was going to do an exchange with dancers from Costa Rica. She was really excited. After writing them back, Nika settled down to read a book Pearl gave her about a beaver kit called Paddy that was found and raised by a man and then released to the wild. The book told how the kit slept in the man's sleeping bag at first, just like Khan. It was hard for Nika to read the part where the kit grew up and swam away.

Maybe seeing her propped on the couch looking bored prompted Ian to decide that this was a perfect time for her to finish her wolf project. He charged into the living room with all her books and papers, and sat with her to check things off, helping her organize her note cards. Sometimes he asked her to write something over if she had done it carelessly, or pointed out something she could explain in greater detail. There were still some charts to be completed recording Khan's growth. Nika thought her science teacher would be impressed.

Finally she was able to limp up the hill to spend time with the growing pup. When she came inside the pen, Khan leaped at the gate. She knew he wanted to run, but her ankle wasn't up to it yet. Besides, would she dare to run with him again? It was hard to imagine doing one more thing that Ian wouldn't like. She was still worried he'd find out they'd released Bristo's animals.

Nika's ankle bruises turned from blue and red to yellow and green, until finally when she laced her boot, the pain was almost gone. It had been a little over a week.

"You're a fast healer," Ian said one morning. "From now on, I'd like you to help with some jobs at the Center. Starting today."

When they arrived at the Center later, Elinor was waiting inside the door. "Nika, want to fly with me today? I'm going to get readings from the collared wolves. You can write down the data on the clipboard."

"Sure." She'd never flown with Elinor before.

"Maybe we'll see some of Khan's relatives from the air," Elinor added with a smile.

Elinor seemed fast and fluttery this morning, as if she was excited about something. "They finished the large enclosure, and I transferred Luna into it this morning." Together Nika and Elinor stuffed vitamins and antibiotics into meatballs, then Elinor said, "Come see!" When they arrived at the tall fence, Luna was lying on the other side. The wolf got up and came over, watching them with her golden eyes. She was thin, but there was little sign that she had been so badly wounded just eight days ago, except for the shaved spot on her shoulder, and the bumpy stitched area of the wound.

Elinor showed Nika how to deliver the meatballs by flattening her hand against the fence, leaving no fingers to get grabbed. Luna neatly devoured the treats, then loped up the hill, where she jumped to the top of a large flat rock and stretched out with her long legs in front of her. Her head was high and proud looking, like a queen on her throne.

"It's big," Nika said as she looked around at Luna's new home. With a heavy heart, she remembered that Khan would occupy the smaller holding pen next.

"I have an errand to do in town. Then we'll drive down to the plane," Elinor said. They climbed into Ian's old kelly green truck, slammed the heavy doors, and turned out of the Center driveway to head toward Main Street.

"We wrote an ad for the *Sentinel*, asking for information about Luna." Elinor parallel-parked in front of the newspaper office, one front tire up on the curb. She needed a few more truck-driving lessons, Nika thought, as they came to rest at an angle.

Elinor handed Nika the ad. "Mind taking it in? Ask for Scott."

Inside the small office, someone in front of the counter was talking in a loud voice. Nika couldn't help but overhear. "Well, I think you should publish more about how dangerous they are. I hate them all, don't care what those tree-huggers say!" The man turned to leave so fast, he bumped into Nika. He gave her a startled look, backed up, and said, "Like your rat's-behind wolf-loving uncle!" Nika flushed and stepped aside, angry and embarrassed.

After the man left, she asked for Scott. A cheerful bearded man came to the counter. He looked apologetic. She handed him the ad, then hurried out of the office and climbed back into the truck.

Elinor slowly pulled out, went down a block, and turned, cutting across the curb at the corner with a bump. Nika held on and asked, "Why do some people hate wolves so much?"

"Yeah, I saw Bart Tyson coming out of the office. It's complicated. Everyone has a right to his feelings. The way I see it is, we have fewer wild spaces, we all get crowded, and some people get to feeling angry and territorial. They worry about their dogs and livestock. Of course, wolves are territorial, too. Dogs are occasionally killed. Deer are killed. People who live with wolves don't always agree about how to manage them."

"So they blame someone like Ian?" Nika said.

"Some people do. And me. We try to find common ground with people like Bart, when we can." Elinor lurched the truck to a stop next to the dock, pulled out the keys, and smiled. "Now, let's go see some wild wolves where they live."

When Maki flashed the Dramamine, Nika grinned and took the package. He gave her a thumbs-up as the yellow plane pulled free from the water, rising quickly over the far shore of Anchor Lake. Elinor took out the blue boxes, set the dials, and handed a box and earphones back to Nika.

"First one is number four-four-nine, a female from Khan's mother's litter three years ago. She's usually up by Little Trout Lake with her pack, miles from any roads. She's black, like Khan."

Pointing, Elinor shouted as they flew, "North from here there are about two million wilderness acres in the BWCAW and the Quetico. They say there are only two major east-west roads between us and the North Pole." It was hard to imagine so few people in all that space.

The plane circled over mirror lakes and dense stands of trees. Suddenly beeps started coming through the earphones. This had been exciting the first time she heard it, but it was even more exciting now. Khan's black sister was down there, living free.

"Looks like three! See them? Resting in that clearing!" Elinor shouted.

Nika nodded, then wrote down the section numbers and lake names that Elinor read off to her. She wrote an

R for "resting." They made five passes. One wolf was black. Two were gray.

"I see another between those rocks!" Nika said, her voice as loud as it would go.

"You're right! Good eye! Another gray!" Elinor shouted, turning to look at Nika. "Okay, we have more collars to check! You okay, Nika?"

Nodding, Nika handed the box forward for Elinor to reset.

When she handed it back, Elinor said, "We wrote a grant for money to start putting GPS collars on some wolves. Then we could sit home and watch them on the computer."

Even if she got sick sometimes, Nika decided this was much more fun.

After getting readings from seven wolves, Elinor signaled to Maki to head back. Nika still didn't love the smelly, churning aircraft, but seeing wild wolves lope across clearings, then melt into heavy forest, made her feel the energy of their freedom in her bones. Of course she couldn't help wishing Khan could be free like his sister.

When they were back in the truck, Elinor asked, "How was that, seeing them where they live?"

There was a mix of sadness and excitement in Elinor's expression. "Cool," Nika answered, realizing that Elinor loved these animals, not as individuals with names and numbers, but just for being the wild creatures that they were.

Elinor drove quietly, bumping over just one corner when she cut it too close. Then, as if she were finishing an unspoken thought, she said, "The best thing we can do for wolves is to allow them space and leave them alone." Nika thought that was a strange thing to say for someone whose job was studying wolves. She was about to ask what she meant when Elinor leaned into the steering wheel, made a sharp turn, and pulled up next to the Center. Ian came strolling out, his face lit up like he'd won the lottery. He leaned into the truck window, very close to Elinor, and the two gave each other a lingering smile.

"I've got a surprise," he said.

The tan wolf sniffed and trotted and marked and scratched. She ran a loop next to the fence, cached a deer leg in the trees, waded in the stream, sat high on her rock. People came to the fence. She danced to see them. But still something was missing. She howled in the night and listened for calls in the wind.

Chapter Twenty

Scoot in back, Nika," Ian said, sliding into the driver's seat and gently pushing Elinor over. The two of them hadn't stopped smiling. "First we have to stop at the Camerons' house in town and pick up Randall."

After they picked him up, Randall sat in the jump seat with Nika while they drove out of town. Minutes later they pulled up in front of a small green house.

"Little Otter Lake. Ours if we want it," Ian announced, making a circle with his hand to include the small house, the dock in front of it, and the lake beyond. What was he talking about? Was this Ian's way of telling them a decision had been made about their future? About their home?

"Wow! Nika, look!" Randall exclaimed as he dove out of the truck and ran toward the house, painted the color of spruce trees.

The house was one story with a giant stone chimney right in front and big windows on both sides.

Ian sounded a little apologetic. "None of the bedrooms are very big." He opened the door to one bedroom that had a sliding window into the screen porch. Across the living room were two more doors, each opening into a room big enough for a bed and not a whole lot more. "We'll have to find some furniture," he said, as though he were thinking out loud.

Randall smiled and ran over and grabbed Nika in a bear hug. "Cool!" was all he managed to say in words, but his face said everything else. He took her by the hand and led her to the doorway of a room that was painted bright blue. "Do you like this one?" he asked.

"No, that's okay. You choose, Randall."

"The blue one," he said, walking to the center of the small room. His eyes jumped around as though, in his fantasies, he had already moved in.

Nika walked over to the window beside the fireplace. In front of the house was a narrow strip of sand beach with grandfather red pines standing on either side. Across the small lake chubby clouds curled over the horizon. It looked pretty good. Is this what she wanted? It would mean leaving Pasadena and Olivia and Zach and what she knew. She wished someone had asked her what she wanted. Deciding something for herself for once in the last two years would have felt so good.

Ian came up beside Nika. "It's a pretty spot, and it's available for two years. It was a vacation cabin, but it's been winterized. They put a furnace in the basement, a specially insulated roof, indoor plumbing . . ." He spoke with excitement.

"Yeah, it's great," she said with a shy smile. She did appreciate what he was trying to do. And Randall was over the moon.

Returning to town, Ian dropped Elinor and Nika at the Center while he took Randall back to the Camerons'. Nika noticed a brand-new sign. The letters carved in shiny yellow pine were freshly painted dark green and said "Center for the Study of Northern Animals." It looked so official.

After they entered through the shiny glass doors, Elinor went back to the kitchenette. "Want a Coke?" she called.

"Sure," Nika answered. She sat down at the big conference table, still thinking about the green house on Little Otter Lake. Everything was all happening so fast. On the table was a memo in Ian's handwriting. She picked it up and started to read:

Well, Nika thought, that's done. She read on.

Khan would be scared. Someone needed to comfort him. She raced through the rest of the list.

Number five gave Nika chills. Was she really never going to be allowed to have contact with Khan again, except through a fence? This was the first she'd heard that Luna could possibly hurt Khan. How could they put the wolves together if they didn't know for sure Khan would be safe?

"Okay, so when's this happening?" Nika asked, waving the paper, when Elinor came in with the Coke. Elinor took the paper from her. As if they hadn't wanted her to see it.

"As you know, Luna has already been transferred. We plan to move Khan next week. Depending on the weather, maybe Wednesday or Friday."

"A week from now!" Nika stood up. "That's too soon!"

"Actually, the timing's just right. Khan will be just over forty pounds, small enough for Luna to think of him as a pup, big enough to stand up to rough play."

Just then Ian came through the door and walked directly to his desk, where he grabbed a ringing phone. While talking, he shuffled through some papers. His movements were quick and businesslike. He seemed preoccupied.

Elinor leaned closer to Nika, saying, "It's really best for Khan and Luna. You'll see."

For a minute Nika felt her throat tighten. She gave Elinor a weak smile, then went out the back door to the pens.

Luna was stretched on the ground in the large enclosure. The tan wolf looked bigger in her new space. Nika plopped against the fence. Never being able to be with Khan, to touch him, to rub his feet, to run with him? Tears filled her eyes to the rims, but she wiped them away. She felt exactly the way she'd never wanted to feel again in her life. Losing a beautiful picture of how things could be. A gentle nibbling on her hair distracted her. She turned to find Luna pressed against the fence behind her, her eyes on Nika, as though she understood.

That night was very hot. Ian wasn't back from town, and Pearl invited Nika to go down with her for a sleepover in the coolness of the screen house by the dock. They carried snacks and blankets, a gas lantern, and books to read. Even on a night like this, they brought hot tea in a thermos. They made their beds on the cots built into the walls of the screen house, unrolling the mattresses that were kept covered when no one was using them.

As they got ready for a swim, with a faraway look Pearl said, "I've been doing this every summer since I can remember. Taking a cooling dip and sleeping in the screen house on hot nights."

When they slipped off the dock, the water seemed cold at first because the air was so hot, but soon it was like no temperature at all. As Nika was treading water, pillows of cold surprised her feet and stars reflected in the glassy water around her. She lay in a back float, amazed by the stillness.

They watched the moon come up like a giant pumpkin, washing out the stars. Moonlight rippled and scattered as they splashed. After they got out and went up to the screen house, the moon climbed the sky, shrinking as it rose.

Soon they settled down on their cots, sharing the wavering light of the gas lamp to read. Nika put down her book and thought for a minute. Pearl had known Ian for a long time.

"Pearl," she said, "do you think Ian is really going to settle down?" After all that had happened, she could easily imagine Ian hitting the road again, given his history.

Pearl answered, "Oh, well. Yes, I think that's what he wants to do."

"Does he really like Elinor?" Nika asked, thinking if he married Elinor, wouldn't they want their own kids?

"I think he does, don't you?"

"Um . . ." It was so complicated.

Just then they heard Ian's boat pull up to the dock, then the creaking sounds of the boatlift, and then soft footsteps coming up the path.

Ian stood by the door of the screen house for a minute. "A perfect night for a moonlight swim. I think I'll take a dip myself."

"How's Luna doing?" Nika asked of his profile in the silvery light of the moon.

"She still likes her new pen, I think. And her shoulder is recovering nicely." Ian took a few steps, then stopped.

He turned and said, "Oh, Nika. One more thing. Sheriff Dunn says he wants to meet with us in the morning. With Thomas and his dad, too." His voice was stone steady, as if he were giving a weather report.

"Okay." She swallowed hard and waited for more. But there wasn't any more. He turned and left. She heard his steps start down the path. In spite of the warm night, she began to shiver.

A minute later she heard the squeak and bang of Ian's cabin door. Soon came another bang, then splashes in the water.

She lay quietly in the light of the hissing lamp, wrapped up tight in her sleeping bag to stop the shivers. The rising and falling notes of a blues guitar coming from Ian's cabin mixed with a riot of loon calls from the lake. Water lapped soft percussion against the rocks.

But the questions started swirling and wouldn't stop. Now what? Would she and Thomas have to go to court? What would happen then?

The next morning, as the big boat cut through the waves, Nika and Thomas sat in the back giving each other brief looks. Randall perched on the edge of Ian's pilot's chair, looking straight ahead, except once when he smirked back at Nika. She found this new side of Randall irritating—he seemed pleased that she was in trouble.

After Ian pulled into his official boat slip in town, Nika and Thomas helped him tie up, then waited for directions. "Now you two go up to the sheriff's office and wait for us." Ian was looking into Nika's eyes. "Jake's coming over from his office at about nine-thirty."

Side by side Nika and Thomas trudged slowly up the hill. When they were out of Ian's hearing, she turned to him. "What do you think will happen?"

"I don't know." Thomas seemed to be thinking. It was one of the things she liked best about him. He was calm and always thought things through his own way. Like when Nika heard about hunters baiting bears with piles of food, she thought it was very unsportsmanlike. But Thomas said he thought it was okay because fewer bears were wounded that way. It helped her think in a new way. Thomas was like that.

"Mom said someone saw us leaving Bristo's that day," said Thomas.

Inside the sheriff's office was a row of wooden chairs beneath a bulletin board bristling with notices tacked up with colored pins. A woman behind a glass shield nodded toward the chairs. They sat down, as keyboards clicked and printers whirred.

It seemed like an hour before the door opened and

Thomas's dad, Jake, and Ian came in, talking comfortably together, even laughing. They stopped talking the minute they saw Thomas and Nika on the chairs. Did Ian and Jake know yet what they'd done?

Seeing the men, the woman behind the glass opened a heavy door and waved them through. They found Sheriff Dunn in a crowded office in the back, his windowsills filled with leggy geranium plants and his chairs and desk covered with files and loose papers.

"Sorry," he said, scraping off two chairs. The woman brought two folding chairs and handed them to Ian, smiling sympathetically. She bustled back in with three cups of steaming coffee on a tray.

Sheriff Dunn had longish eyebrows, red hair, and a sandy beard. After looking at Ian and Jake, he pulled a set of wire cutters from a drawer and put them on the desk. He leaned toward Nika and Thomas. "So, am I wrong in guessing that you two were the ones who released Bristo's animals earlier in the summer?" he said.

Ian shot to his feet. Jake rubbed his eyebrows with one hand and said, "Thomas?" Sheriff Dunn held up his hand to the two men like a traffic cop. Ian sat back down.

Thomas spoke first. "Except for the wolf. Luna. We don't know how she got out."

Nika sat up straight. "It was all my idea. I think it's wrong to keep wild animals in cages." Even though she was scared, the words just came out. She looked into the eyes of the sheriff.

Sheriff Dunn took a sip of his coffee. "You know, Bristo gets all worked up about things. He can't totally help the way he is. And you're right—he doesn't treat animals very well." His voice was low and firm. "Authorities have been dealing with him for years." He paused, then stood and moved some papers aside and perched on the edge of his messy desk. "Probably Bristo wouldn't be in jail right now if you kids hadn't released his animals."

"Except what would have happened to those animals? Their cages were cramped. They looked starved. He was mean," Nika blurted. She surprised herself, speaking up like this.

"Protecting those animals wasn't a job for you kids."

Nika glanced to see Ian's arms crossed in front of him.

She looked down and said more quietly, "It seems to me, no one has ever done much about his mistreatment of animals."

"You should have shared your concern!" Ian said abruptly, leaning forward. He and Jake met each other's eyes.

"And what would have happened if I did?" Her voice thickened in her throat. Why wasn't he standing up for her? Hurt rose within her. "Isn't Bristo the one who shot Khan's mother? Why didn't someone arrest him then?"

The sheriff shifted to look directly at Nika. "Well, now someone has arrested him. And the charges are serious—shooting the wolf and endangering you kids. We're hoping the judge will order treatment this time."

He continued on with his quiet, steady voice. "So. For restitution for the vandalism, it's all set up for both of you to do community service at the Greenstone Home for Seniors. I'll decide the number of hours. How does that sound?"

Both Nika and Thomas nodded silently.

"Okay, then." He emptied his cup and nodded at Ian and Jake. "Sound okay to you?"

Both men leaned back and nodded.

Nika's feelings were helter-skelter. At least mopping floors and sorting magazines was better than going to court. On the other hand, it scared her to be around people who were really sick or old. She was afraid something might happen to them. But Thomas was sort of smiling. What was that about?

"All right, then. Just the thing." Sheriff Dunn pounded his paper-covered desk with his fist. He gave them a quick smile and reached out to shake hands with Nika and Thomas. Jake and Ian stood but made no effort to leave the office.

"Nika, why don't you head back to the Center? Elinor and Randall should be there," Ian said.

"Thomas, go straight to the dock," Jake said. "I'll be down in a bit. You've got jobs to do at home."

When they burst out of the door, Nika grabbed Thomas's arm to slow him down. "You're smiling. Why are you smiling?"

Thomas said, "Just 'cause we lucked out, I guess."

"So what's so great about working in the nursing home?" she asked.

Thomas held out both hands palms up and shrugged with one shoulder. "I just like old people." He snatched a glance at the pies in the window of the Busy Bee, then looked at her and smiled. "He could have asked us to clear prickly invasive plants from the roadsides, haul rocks, or dig outhouses," he said. "Think of that."

Nika thought clearing invasive plants might be okay. The two of them didn't talk much as they continued back through town.

When they neared the tall trees at the edge of the Center's property, Thomas stopped. "I've got some stuff to do. See you later."

"No, no," Nika pleaded. "Come with me." Right now she didn't want to be alone.

"Uh-uh. Sorry. You heard my dad," Thomas answered, accelerating into a jog.

Suddenly the air was filled with scents that the silvery-tan wolf knew deep in her body's memory. She sorted the layers of her senses and trotted over to peer through the fence. There she saw the familiar humans huddled together looking at something, their backs to her. The tan wolf scraped the ground, parted her lips, then sniffed again.

Chapter Twenty-One

After the meeting in the sheriff's office, Ian seemed even more intent on keeping Nika busy with her project, or with jobs at the Center. Maybe he was trying to get her used to life without the growing black pup. A routine developed. Each morning after she fed Khan, she had to meet Ian in front of his cabin for their ride to town. Volunteers were spending more and more time with the pup. Ian thought it was important for Khan to accept care from a variety of people. In Nika's opinion, too many people. Khan was slipping away from her, Ian was still pretty mad about Bristo's, and now everyone in town would know that she had been ordered to do community service in restitution for vandalism.

When she arrived at Ian's cabin on Tuesday morning, he was still inside. She knocked and peeked in. He was at his laptop writing.

"C'mon in," he said. She opened the door and stepped inside.

It had been almost a week, and she still hadn't brought up number five from Ian's list. She'd wanted things to settle down a bit after their visit to the sheriff.

"Looks like Friday will be moving day," Ian said. "Just a sec. I have to finish this. Did you eat?"

"Pearl sent these." She unwrapped two blueberry muffins from a napkin and looked around for a plate to put them on, or at least a paper towel. "Do you have any dishes? I'll get something."

"Frills," he said, picking up a muffin. "Looks delicious. Thanks." She guessed after being a bachelor so long, he'd developed casual habits.

He took a bite and looked back at his computer screen, where columns of numbers trooped across the page. "Plans for the Center. Budgets for buildings and enclosures and what not. Not my favorite chore."

Nika looked around. His cabin was messy, with packs, books, radio parts, reports, and tools scattered across every surface. In the food area, a single jar of trail mix rested on a stack of books. CDs were stacked in uneven piles beside his CD player. Old blues, Scott Joplin, classical. Two guitars hung from pegs on the wall.

His clothes were neatly folded on the unpainted wood shelves of an open closet in the corner. A small couch with leaf print fabric sat by itself on a bright red and orange foreign-looking rug in the center of the room. In one corner was a bed. Against the back wall was a pot-bellied wood stove with curvy legs crouched on a platform of bricks. With its almost-human shape, it seemed like it should have a name, like Gertrude.

Nika was avoiding the subject that was festering. She picked a piece of muffin off the front of her shirt.

She wanted to say something, but her words vaporized. Her face must have shown how she stopped herself from speaking.

"What's up?" Ian asked. He stacked his papers, packed his computer in a case, and gathered his socks and boots.

She plopped down on the small couch and ran her hand over the faded green fabric. "Well, okay . . ." She shrugged and tried to force a smile, but it stiffened up. "So why can't I ever be with Khan again, after he's in with Luna?"

Ian walked slowly over to the couch, dropped his boots onto the floor, and sat next to her. They were both silent. Then he shifted to face her. "We all have to have rabies shots to be with the animals after they are in the Center. Then we don't know about Luna, yet—socialized wolves can be more dangerous than wild wolves."

"But you never told me I couldn't be with Khan. In the big pen. I only know because I found your list at the Center." Her voice got very quiet. "It's like I don't matter."

"Of course you matter, and I'm sorry if you think—" Ian put his head back and took a deep breath. "I never should have done this, let you help raise the pup." It was as though he were talking to himself. "I thought it would be a way for us to . . . well, to work together, get to know each other. It was a mistake. I didn't realize you might, well, that the pup might—"

Anger brought her to her feet, and she turned to face him.

"That I might love him and want to keep him? Is that what you mean?" What did he expect when he'd handed her a helpless pup and asked her to hold it close?

"Look, Nika. You haven't made this easy." He stood up and paced barefoot. "First, you decide to take Khan without a leash, knowing I wouldn't approve."

"I just wanted him to know what it felt like, to be free like a wild wolf."

"That wasn't your decision to make."

"Obviously," she threw back.

"And you almost lost Khan. Then I find out you and Thomas released Bristo's animals and are in trouble with the sheriff. Again, deciding to do something you both knew your families wouldn't like."

"We're doing community service to pay back for that!"

Ian's face was red. "As if this weren't enough, then you feed a wolf, and that wolf gets shot!"

"Shooting the wolf wasn't because we fed her. She might have died! It was Bristo!" Didn't he understand? It was because of them that Luna was alive!

"You endangered yourselves. You figured she was Bristo's runaway, and you knew the man had shown threatening behavior before. No one should ever feel certain that a wolf is totally safe. Finally, you went there just as a storm was brewing, instead of coming home. None of this shows good judgment. How can I trust you?" Ian threw his hands up in a helpless gesture.

"Well then, maybe you should just send me home, if I'm that much trouble."

"Oh, Nika," Ian said, half groaning and turning toward his desk.

Nika charged out the door, slamming it behind her. She felt sick as she ran to the dock. A fight like this was new to her. There'd been a girl in her second foster home who liked to hit and seemed to wait for Nika around every corner. Nika had hit her back once, hard. She remembered the sound. It didn't feel good, even though the girl deserved it. But this was different. This felt dangerous. It felt as if, just by getting mad, she could lose everything.

o o o

That night was still and dry. Nika's sleeplessness became a net for every sound: loons, the scuffling of small rodents, the short barking call of an owl. The fight with Ian kept rolling over and over in her mind. It was so confusing. There was only one thing that could make her feel better.

After Pearl was in bed and Ian had gone down to his cabin on the beach, she collected the old raggedy sleeping bag and followed the moon up the path, not even using a flashlight. The night was cloudless. Inside the pen, as she slid into the bag, she felt a mist of dew settle on the nylon. Khan came to nestle quietly beside her as though agreeing with the need for stealth. His eyes sparked in the moonlight, and she felt his breath against her arm. Most of the night the wolf slept. Most of the night she didn't.

When she woke at dawn, Khan was gone. She didn't want to get up. Maybe if she never crawled out of her sleeping bag into the thin light of the soundless morning, nothing would change. The warmth of Khan beside her at midnight would never cool, and every morning forever the wolf would greet her like a wave smoothly running to shore.

But then, if she didn't get up, they couldn't have a last run. She'd planned not to run with Khan again, because of Ian. But then they had argued, and she figured she'd never have another opportunity in her whole life. Just one more time. She pulled herself out of the sleeping bag and slipped out of the gate to visit the outhouse. On her way back she picked up meat scraps from the fridge.

Back in the pen, she put the scraps on a rock and waited. The agile pup, now weighing nearly forty-two pounds at fourteen weeks old, trotted down to accept his gift. After a quick greeting, Nika opened the gate, and Khan lengthened his smooth black shape to bullet down the path.

Today, instead of disappearing or playing hide and seek, Khan ran circles around her as they walked. He bumped his head under her hand and once took her hand in his mouth and pulled as if he wanted her to play. She stopped, said "No!" then pushed him over on his back, having to be forceful and use both hands. He squirmed, and when he quieted, she rubbed his belly.

They went to the rendezvous spot as usual, where they watched the blaze of early sun cut through the trees like stage lights. On the way back they stopped and searched for any blueberries that might be still ripening on the ridge. Khan picked berries the way he often ate, lying down. He picked delicately with his teeth. *This is what I'll remember,* Nika thought. *I could be a cave girl or an early Native American girl or an old woman, and it would be the same—two creatures together, feeling freedom and connection to the plants and rocks and scents surrounding them.* Ian had told her that one single underground root system made one huge organism of connected aspen trees as big as seventy-five football fields. With Khan she felt like she was a part of something like that now.

The changing light told her it was time to get back. Ian and Elinor were probably waiting.

Elinor lured Khan into his old plastic baby kennel with morsels of moose meat. Nika rushed to the pen for the sleeping bag and what was left of the old stuffed bear, then trailed the caravan led by Maki and Ian carrying the kennel down to the dock. In the boat she sat on the floor next to the covered kennel and crooned to Khan as they crossed the unwrinkled waters of Anchor Lake. Once they came ashore, she stayed with him again in the back of the pickup, until they all crowded into the room-size holding pen at the Center. No one talked much. Elinor and Maki went back inside, leaving Ian and Nika with a heavily panting Khan. With his ears back in worried position, he looked small and scared.

Soon Khan panted less and accepted water. Being so focused on the pup, Nika had forgotten all about Luna. Then she heard the whimpers, almost like pup-whimpers. Luna was lying with her legs straight out in front of her, facing the rolling gate between the enclosure and the holding pen. Her eyes fixed on Khan's kennel as she emitted a groan, then whimpered again, her jaws dripping as though she had her eye on a tasty treat. Ian had said something about the hormone prolactin and how it made adult wolves feel parental. He nodded and let Khan out of the kennel. The pup curled his body as he rushed over to the fence. Luna growled and Khan turned on his back. Did this mean Luna might hurt Khan? Ian and Elinor smiled at each other and returned to the Center, saying they all needed to give the wolves some time to adjust. Nika tucked down in the back corner of the holding pen to watch.

Later when the wolves were calmly lying on either side of the fence, Nika got up to go back inside. As she approached the Center door, she saw two figures in the window of the office. They were facing each other. She slowed to a stop. Then the two figures came together and kissed. It was Ian and Elinor.

A whirlwind of feeling came over her. She went out the other gate and hurried toward the parking lot, her face burning. She would wait for Ian in the truck.

After a while, Ian came through the Center doors, looking puzzled. He walked to the passenger side of the truck where she was slumped in the seat.

"Where did you go? We want to show you something. We've been waiting."

Nika shrugged. *We!*

Ian put his hand on the truck door handle, pausing, as though trying to figure out what was going on now. Then, with a no-nonsense look on his face, he opened the door, took her arm, and gently pulled her from the truck. "You've got to see this." He kept his hand on her arm all the way into the building, as though she would suddenly bolt down the street. Which was possible, in the mood she was in.

They marched through the office and out the back door, where they stopped by the holding pen. Both wolves were at the fence, but this time Khan was chewing on something between his front feet. Luna stood on the other side of the fence, looking down, strings of drool falling from her lips. The object Khan was chewing on was a raw chicken.

"Luna gave him a gift," Ian said quietly. "She dug a hole under the gate and pushed the chicken into it until Khan could grab hold and pull it through."

"Wow," said Nika. "Are you sure?"

"Yup," Ian answered, smiling. "Elinor watched. Luna worked away at it for about fifteen minutes."

So maybe Khan had found his pack. Nika should be glad for him. Ian was. And because she wasn't entirely, she felt selfish.

But in a way it made her decision easier.

The silvery-tan wolf wore a pathway in the grass beside the smaller pen. When she gazed at the pup, saliva filled her mouth, and an urge came over her. She wanted the pup to be closer, to taste his breath in her mouth, to run beside him through the trees.

Chapter Twenty-Two

In the pale green light after sunset, Ian and Nika pulled up to Pearl's dock. Nika jumped from the boat and held the ropes while Ian got out. The sound of the ratchets in the lift crank usually meant to her that everyone was home and safe, but tonight the sound brought no comfort. She felt tired. She dragged her feet the last bit up the darkening path to Pearl's. All she wanted right now was to be alone in her room to absorb the loss of Khan, and the new image of Elinor and Ian together.

As they came through the door of Pearl's, Nika headed straight for the stairs.

Pearl was knitting in a pool of light from a small reading lamp. "I've got some chicken wild rice soup," she said. Ian smiled at Pearl and went straight through into the kitchen.

Nika said, "Oh. Thanks. But maybe later." She made an effort to smile as she stood at the bottom of the steps. As a reflex, she thought, *I should go up and check on Khan.* Then she remembered. The pen was empty. She almost felt like going anyway, but Pearl and Ian would be watching, feeling sorry for her. Sympathy was not what she needed right now.

Almost the whole time Nika had been in Pearl's house, Khan had been here as well. It felt so strange.

Nika had to change gears. She had to pump herself up with enough strength to make a giant choice, her choice, to take a giant risk. She dove into her messy closet to look for the cash she'd been keeping for emergencies. It should be with her return ticket, inside a large manila envelope. At first she didn't find the envelope and panicked. Finally, she found it in a carry-on bag buried at the back. She transferred the ticket and cash to her backpack, along with her student ID, a few clothes, and her journal. She found the wolf logs with the report she'd written, and threw them in. She climbed up onto her bunk to get her family photos and the ones Thomas had taken of her with Khan on the Big Island. Then she crammed in a few more clothes and a toothbrush. When everything was ready, she shoved the backpack into the closet. If someone asked about it in the morning, she would say it was her wolf project she needed to finish.

After some clattering in the kitchen, Nika heard footsteps go out onto the porch. Pearl and Ian were probably having their evening tea. They talked longer than usual, their voices murmuring like a river over rocks. Finally Ian called up the stairs, "See you in the morning, Nika."

After a few minutes quiet footsteps ascended the stairs. "I've brought some soup and cornbread," Pearl said through the door.

Nika slid from her bunk and opened the door. "Thanks, Pearl," she said, taking the tray and smiling. Thank goodness for Pearl. Nika's stomach had been turning inside out. No one could fool Pearl.

Her hunger gone, Nika tried to sleep, but she kept hearing the fierce whistling of the wind in the eaves. Khan was afraid of the wind. What would he think in his new pen, with no place familiar to hide?

In the morning, after eating oatmeal she found in a pan on the stove, Nika gathered up her overstuffed backpack and met Ian at the dock. The sky was like a faded gray sweater today, soft and dull and close. In Red Pine, before he inserted the key in the ignition of the truck, he turned to look at her.

"I know this is hard. Remember, you can always visit

the wolves privately at the fence, as long as you're out of sight of the visitors."

This was a long way from running with Khan on the Big Island. As they drove to the Center, Nika gripped the door handle tightly, and didn't respond.

"Of course, we still need them to be accustomed to some handling, for vet checks or maintaining health, but mostly we want them to live as natural a life as possible while captive."

"Why even socialize them if you can't hang out with them?"

"I've told you before, Nika. The socializing is for the wolves, not for us. So we can care for them, so they won't be stressed out by people."

"I guess it doesn't matter." Nika closed the truck door and with a backwards wave, she headed off to the Greenstone Home for Seniors. Thomas had been right. Volunteering with seniors was much better than she'd expected.

Later, back at the Center with her back against Luna's fence, Nika sat beside Khan, maybe for the last time. He was lying on his side in the shade of a large pine branch someone had propped up for him. Nika thought about wire cutters. How great it had been to watch the foxes escape from Bristo's! She wished she could do that for these two, even though she knew that what Thomas said was true—they wouldn't last long on their own.

She watched Khan's flank rising and falling. She felt tears begin to build. Without her consent, they began to roll down her cheeks. Khan tilted his head back to look at her face. Soon he was on his feet, watching her.

"I guess they're not going to let me take care of you anymore," she said, looking into his golden eyes.

Khan came very close and stood quietly, the sun heating his black coat under her hand. She took a deep breath and wiped her nose on her sleeve.

"You'll have Luna, that's the main thing, someone who talks wolf and plays rough and runs with you. And you'll have tasty roadkill. No one will shoot you. You'll have Dave if you get sick." Khan turned to the fence, his eyes trained on the dense trees that hid the back portion of the large enclosure. Luna must be back there. Nika knew it was impossible to read his wolf mind, but when he cocked his head to look and listen, she imagined he was wondering about his new life, too.

When Ian and Elinor came out to the holding pen, Elinor was holding a yellow sticky note in her hand.

"More surprises, Nika," she said, briefly leaning down to rub Nika's shoulders, as her mother might have done. "We got an e-mail in response to that ad. A woman about fifty miles from here lost her captive female wolf in a storm last spring. A tree crushed the fence, and the wolf escaped. I called her. Her description sounds just like Luna."

"Is she going to take her back?" Nika jumped to her feet, alarmed. She really didn't want this to happen. She was just beginning to accept that Khan and Luna would be together.

"The neat thing is that she sounded pretty happy to hear about our situation here and says she'd like to donate Luna to the Center, with visiting privileges. I think she found out that keeping a wolf as a pet was harder than she thought."

On her walk to town, Nika looked at her watch. The online schedule said the bus left at 4:40 every day except Sunday. It was just past noon, so she had plenty of time to get the ticket and head back to the Center for one last goodbye with the wolves. She'd even have time to buy a sandwich, though how she would ever eat again was a mystery. Her stomach fluttered and churned like a fishbowl full of minnows.

Downtown Red Pine wasn't big, but she still didn't know where the bus depot was. She'd seen it but couldn't remember exactly what street. Nervously, she asked in the drugstore, and a lady with a hairpiece on crooked gave her a funny look, cracked her gum, and said, "Over a block on Chatfield, next to the lumberyard."

The small beige office of the bus depot was bare except for a few yellow plastic chairs. Nika walked up to a window and waited. Finally a man in a beige uniform came over. "Yeauhh?"

"How much for a ticket to Minneapolis?"

"How many?" He asked.

"One"

"One way?"

"Yes, please."

He shot her a look with narrowed eyes and told her the amount. "That includes tax." She hoped he wouldn't call anyone.

"Oh, yeah, okay." She pulled the money envelope from her backpack and counted it out. She was so glad she'd saved last year when she was walking Rookie. She had $108 left after paying for the bus, mostly in fives and one-dollar bills.

"By yourself?" the agent said as he handed her the ticket, giving her another one of those looks.

"Going to see my aunt. Thanks." Nika lifted her chin.

"You know what time?" asked the depot man.

"Four-forty, right?"

"Yes. Four-forty p.m. Same time, Monday through Saturday."

"Thanks, again," she called over her shoulder as she went out the door.

In the gas station closest to the bus depot, all the food looked petrified with sugar and chemicals, but she bought some homemade cookies, a couple of ready-made sandwiches, and two apples. It would have to do. She was all set now, except for one detail. She was planning to stay at Olivia's, but she'd never received a letter back from her. Olivia was probably busy with soccer practice and dance, or maybe the letter got lost. She looked at the clock over the counter. There was plenty of time for one more trip to the post office, to see if a letter had come.

Standing in the stone-floored post office, she sorted through the mail for Little Berry Island and found a letter with her name on it. She knew it! Olivia had written just in time! She put the rest of the mail back into the box, along with three envelopes that she pulled from her backpack. One for Ian, one for Randall, and one for Pearl. Last night it had seemed like the right thing to write letters. Now she wished she'd written one to Thomas, too, and Elinor. Oh well, she could always write from California. She left her key inside the P.O. box and snapped it shut. When she looked more closely at the letter she'd received, she saw Meg's swirly handwriting. It wasn't from Olivia, she thought with disappointment. But it would be great to have Meg's letter to read on the bus. Maybe Meg was feeling better. She stuffed it in the front flap of her pack.

She probably should have tried calling Olivia, but she would have had to call from the Center, and she hadn't wanted anyone to overhear her plans. If it turned out that she couldn't stay with Olivia and her mom very long, or Meg, she could probably stay with Zach's family. Olivia's mom was really nice, though. She'd always hugged Nika and joked with her. She was sure it would work. Then, later, she could go back to Meg's. Nika was old enough not to need actual parents anymore. She just needed a place to stay. And to finish school. When she thought about it, it all seemed perfectly sensible.

The silvery-tan wolf surveyed the humans from her greeting rock as they stirred in and out of the black wolf's pen. Energy sparked in the air. What would happen now? At last the tan wolf could not stay still and raced into the deep trees of the pen and back again. The black wolf that she wanted to know stood watching her, then looked at the humans, then watched her again.

Chapter Twenty-Three

There was one last thing to do. Nika carried her heavy backpack into the Center and placed it under a desk. She had to say goodbye to Khan, and she had to be there when Khan joined Luna.

She ran into Ian as he and Elinor were heading out to the pens. "Good, you're here. It's time." She nodded and the three of them clanged into the holding pen.

"We'll slide the gate open, and the wolves will decide what to do," Ian said. "Luna can come into the holding pen or Khan can join her. Then Elinor and I will spend time in the pen with them, to make sure everything's okay."

Did Khan know he was saying goodbye? Nika wondered. When she moved to leave the holding pen, he leaped up on her, reaching high with his paws, saying *wowrrr* almost as a howl, then spun toward the closed gate where Luna stood, her ears pricked forward.

After everyone left Khan's pen and the gate rolled open, Luna rushed in, scrambling to a stop in front of Khan. For a moment both wolves became statues. Khan rolled in submission. Luna buried her nose in his fur. Then she bent her front legs in a play bow, her rump high, and streaked into the large enclosure. Khan raced at her side, grabbing at the fur of her shoulder.

The older wolf ran to the top of the mound above the den, where she watched the young black pup approach. Ian had reminded Nika that at this point, if Luna chose to hurt Khan, which could happen, there was nothing anyone could do.

Khan sniffed around some bushes, urinated in a squat, and finally walked closer to the mound where Luna stood. His ears were tipped forward. He stood very tall, looking intently at Luna. Even with his gangly, half-grown body, Nika could see the adult wolf beginning to emerge in his posture. Ian had said in three more months he would be nearly the size of Luna. *A very big pup,* she thought, looking at Luna. He was beautiful but she missed the round-bellied baby pup that had snuggled up to her.

Suddenly Luna leaped to zigzag and dash across the

enclosure. The lameness in her leg didn't show at all now when she ran, reminding Nika what Ian always said, that wolves are tough. Streams of sunlight caught in Luna's coat, bringing out the colors of her fur, all the colors of wolf. Why were they called gray wolves, Nika wondered again, when they came in so many colors—black, golden tan in spots, tweedy gray, lighter tan, white? Luna was very light, but she still had a saddle of gray across her shoulders. Watching them run, Nika kept swallowing down the lump in her throat.

Khan raced behind her, and then they stopped to sniff each other's faces. Again Luna bounded away, this time until she was out of sight in the trees. Khan followed her in a rolling lope and disappeared as well. In a few minutes the two of them came racing full speed, shoulder to shoulder, circling the open area and disappearing back into the trees. Once when they skidded to a stop, Nika saw Luna loop her front leg over Khan's back.

When she did that, both Elinor and Ian laughed. Apparently all the right wolf language was being expressed and understood.

Nika stood watching the two penned wolves splayed side by side on the mound atop the new den, as though they'd been together forever. It was about as happy and sad a scene as Nika could imagine. She turned away from them and left quickly. She couldn't let anything soften her resolve now.

In the office, she found Ian at his computer. "I'm going into town for a bit," she said. She noticed a newly framed photo on his desk beside his computer. It was a picture of the three of them at Serpent Lake with a giant pot full of blueberries. They were all laughing because he'd had to reset his camera timer three times to catch the shot.

"Be back here by six," Ian said, tapping away.

"Okay, well. 'Bye, Ian," she said, grabbing her backpack on her way out the door. He didn't even seem to hear her. He seemed happy today. Like all was well with the world.

They ran shoulder to shoulder. With her controlled bite, she held his fur. She held his muzzle in her mouth, then sniffed him when he rolled. It was as though he had always been with her. And when they waited and watched, they waited and watched within the territory of each other's sight or smell or hearing.

Chapter Twenty-Four

Nika tapped her foot nervously on the gray painted concrete floor as she waited on one of the yellow plastic chairs. Her ticket stuck out of a pocket on the side of her backpack, right where she could keep her eye on it. Every few minutes she glanced at the door, half expecting Ian to storm in and point a finger, directing her to his green truck. Finally she heard the rumble of the bus. The time had come to line up in front of the small, sand-colored building.

Several people carried bags from the parking lot, tickets in their hands. Nika found herself in a line of seven or eight people. When it was her turn, she gave her ticket to a short man in a uniform shirt, his large middle folding over his belt. He tore the ticket and gave her back a stub.

"Want me to put that bag somewheres?" He nodded toward the underside of the bus, where bags were being loaded.

"No, thanks," she said, and climbed into the half-empty bus, clutching her bulging backpack to her chest.

"Take a seat, everyone. This ain't a trolley!" chanted the uniformed man as he swung into the driver's seat. Going down the aisle, Nika passed a man in a baseball cap with his head bent over a newspaper, an elderly woman in a pink and yellow dress unwrapping a dripping sandwich, two middle-aged couples.

She couldn't make herself choose a seat. She just stood in the aisle toward the back, looking around at these people she didn't know.

The bus driver squeaked the door shut and shouted back, "Once more, everybody. Take a seat or take your chances!"

The long seat across the back looked okay, behind a mother and her two kids. Nika bumped her way down the aisle and sat just as the bus lurched and groaned out of the parking lot. The engine whined up and down through the gears as it stopped at cross streets. As it left the edges of the town, it picked up speed, humming down the highway. She would really miss Khan. But in a thunderclap sort of way, she understood. Maybe she'd always known what had to happen but just didn't want to admit it. Still she was deeply sorry he wouldn't get to live in a faraway forest with his own pack, sorry they couldn't always run together on the Big Island.

It seemed to Nika they were going awfully fast. They passed the Log House just beyond the edge of town. Ian had taken them there for homemade ice cream. Next was the egg farm, where they always got organic eggs. The eggshells were green or brown, the yolks almost orange. Past the egg farm was a turnoff to a waterfall, where Ian had taken them to swim. It was strange. She hadn't been here that long, but everything along this road was as familiar as her home street in Pasadena, except everything here was far apart with spruce bogs and stands of trees in between.

Nika realized she was clutching her pack so tightly, her hands hurt. She released her grip and set the backpack beside her on the empty seat. She reminded herself again why she was riding on this noisy bus with strangers, leaving a place she had begun to love. Randall had a home now and didn't need her anymore. Luna was safe from Bristo. Khan would bond with Luna. Ian and Elinor would live happily ever after. No one here needed her.

As the bus settled into a monotone hum, they passed more familiar sights: the burned-over area from a forest fire, the swamp where the spruces looked like old worn-out toothbrushes, the turnoff to the casino on Half-way Bay.

She tried to relax into the rhythms of the bus. Soon she noticed that a girl was staring over the seat in front of her. She was maybe seven years old and leaned both arms on the back of the seat. The girl's mom and brother were sitting one seat ahead of the girl. Nika had passed them when boarding, so they must already have been on the bus when it stopped. The little girl shifted to dangle a ragged teddy bear from one hand, fingering its worn ears and sucking the thumb of the other hand. The brother shot the girl mean looks from time to time over the back of his seat, and the mother was in some kind of hys-terics, rattling on nonstop and talking at the girl about talking when she shouldn't, making them late, being a tattletale. Nika couldn't hear everything the mother said, only the words when she turned her head. The girl never looked at her family but stared at Nika, curling down-ward until only her eyes and the bear showed over the seat back.

Suddenly, the girl jumped up and came back to the bench seat and plunked down hard a little distance away from Nika still clutching the bear. Nika wanted to com-fort her, to tell her to be strong. She smiled at the girl and said, "That's a nice bear. What's his name?"

When the girl turned and looked at her, there was angry fire in her eyes. She said, "Stop looking at me."

Her forehead wrinkled, and her eyes reminded Nika of the cougar at Bristo's. Nika felt sad for this girl who seemed so alone at such a young age. Her dark eyes and neatly pulled-back black shiny hair would have made her pretty, but she wasn't. Her face was an angry mask.

Nika wondered what she could do for her. She offered the girl a chocolate chip cookie from her backpack. "Here, do you want one of these?"

The girl pinned Nika with her eyes again and said, "Leave me alone."

Nika was confused. Why had the girl moved to the bench seat next to her, then acted like Nika had taken a swing at her with stick?

She placed the cookie on a clean napkin she'd found in the pocket of her pack and gave the girl a little smile. She pushed it halfway, like you would put out seeds for a nervous chipmunk.

She took out a cookie for herself, then remembered Meg's letter in the pocket of her backpack. Hopefully Meg was better. Perhaps Meg had talked to Olivia's mom.

Dear Nika,

It was so good to get your letter describing how you helped raise the little wolf puppy. You have obviously found a new and exciting world to explore. I would love to see that pup, although, he's probably not very small anymore. I loved the pictures your friend Thomas took of him and have put them on my refrigerator.

I have a couple of things to say. One is about the impression that I got from your letter that you didn't think staying there would work and how much you looked forward to coming back to California. I was confused, because everything and everyone you talked about sounded wonderful, like good people to be with. So this is my advice, whether you want it or not. If you love a place, it's home. If people love you, they are family. Family can come in many shapes and forms. But first you must open your heart before you can really know how much other people care about you. My feeling is that you've just started to do that. It's tempting, when you have lost as much as you have, to think you have to be perfect for things to go right, to belong, to be loved. I wonder if maybe you have already found what you need?

So, enough lecture from your old friend Meg. You know I love you and will always be happy to see you, but my life has changed, too. The doctors say I will be fine, but that I must give up being a foster mom for good. Whenever this makes me sad, which it does, of course, all I have to do is think of each of you off finding lives of your own and how I offered you hugs and a safe place to help you get strong again.

You and Randall are welcome to visit anytime. I know your friends will be happy to see you, too.

Love, Meg

The letter fell to Nika's lap as a rush of air left her lungs. She could never go back to live at Meg's. Ever again. And not one word about Olivia.

The bus seemed to be going faster and faster. Too fast. Her throat ached. What was she doing?

She looked again at the hardened face of the little girl, and at the uneaten cookie on the napkin between them, and with a shock Nika realized what Meg said in her letter was right. She still missed her mom so much, but now she would be missing Randall and Ian and Khan. And she realized that if she was willing, she could trust Ian and work things through. They could become a human pack, a family. It was up to her.

Suddenly nothing about this bus ride was right. Yesterday, it made sense but it didn't make sense anymore. It was just like when Nika lived with Meg. Her foster mom had always been able to say things in few words that helped her see the truth inside. A burst of joyful craziness swept over her as the bus careened down the highway, and she leaped to her feet. She reached into her backpack again and pulled out the brown paper sack. She picked up the uneaten cookie from the seat, put it in with the others, and leaned over. She held out the whole sack of cookies to the girl.

"Thanks," Nika told her. "You don't know it, but I think you just saved my life. Take these. You might want them later. Don't give up. Take care." Still scowling the girl looked up at her with a wrinkled forehead, but accepted Nika's gift with both hands.

The motion of the bus made it hard to walk, but Nika zigzagged to the front and tapped the bus driver on the shoulder. She shouted over the motor noise. "Stop! Can you stop, please?"

The driver cut his eyes in her direction but didn't slow the bus. "Next town's twenty miles, I stop there." He reached over to turn up the volume on his radio.

"I'm going to be sick all over the bus," Nika said loudly, fixing him with her eyes.

His head snapped around, eyes wide with alarm.

"Really, really sick," she said as she leaned slightly toward him, wincing, one hand at her throat, one on her stomach. "I do this all the time, get very sick on buses. It's awful. Once I start, I just can't seem to stop. I feel it coming, right now . . ." She gagged and grabbed the railing.

The bus lurched and stuttered and moaned down through the gears, jerking to a stop, pulling onto the shoulder by a driveway. The door wheezed open.

Nika waved at the girl in the back row, hoisted her backpack, and shot out the door.

"How'll you get back?" the irritated driver barked before closing the door.

More she couldn't hear. The door closed with a hiccup, and the bus rumbled away. Tears rivered quietly down her face. Happy tears. Meg would be proud. Mom, too.

As the bus disappeared over the hill in a grind of gears and a trail of exhaust, she wondered how many miles back to town. The sun's heat captured in the asphalt radiated up through her feet. She looked at the open blue sky, the tall pines striped with late afternoon light. Even with brush at the roadside drying and brown, and a horse-fly dive bombing at her head, it was like a postcard, her postcard. As she squatted to tie her sneaker, she heard the sound of a car. A truck was coming down the highway from Red Pine, a truck moving very, very fast. *The sheriff should give him a ticket,* she thought. But before she could stand up, the truck raced by in a flash of familiar kelly green. Soon it was plummeting over the far hill. A truck hot on the tail of a lumbering bus.

Relief pulled Nika to her feet, a solid feeling like after a long swim when you get close to the shore and suddenly your feet touch the bottom. It didn't even matter if they were mad at her for leaving. Or if they yelled at her. Except that now they were disappearing over a faraway hill.

Nika laughed. She'd finally made her decision, and Ian had raced right by, not even seeing her. Maybe he would chase the bus all the way to Minneapolis. She pictured Ian forcing the bus to stop, then having to listen to a few choice words from the cranky bus driver.

Time stopped. Then after forever, the kelly green truck came crawling slowly back over the hill. She waved and jumped, and waved again and jumped some more. The truck sped up, then looped in a U-turn, spitting up dust as it pulled onto the sandy shoulder behind her. Ian leaped out almost before the truck stopped. Elinor's red hair flashed as she threw open her door. Randall struggled out from the cramped second seat.

Nika walked, then ran toward the truck. Running toward now, not running away. When you only had a few pieces left in a puzzle, once you saw those last pieces, you knew exactly where they fit.

Epilogue

It was deep winter, tree shadows inked by moonlight on fresh snow. The silvery-tan wolf lifted her nose. Coming to the fence were the girl-like-the-woman and the smaller boy, the tall man who talked calmly, the woman who gave meat. The tan wolf leaped to stand on the greeting rock, her tail at ease.

When the girl-like-the-woman and the tall man clanged through the gate into the enclosure, the almost full-grown black pup bounced across the snow to greet them, his tall body twisting, his tail loose and circling.

After the humans went back through the gate, the tan wolf heard a low and rising sound, then another. The black pup ran to lick the tan wolf's lips, to bow before her. They stood, shoul-

ders touching, ears pricked forward. Now all four humans blended their voices in a howl, a little like wolves, but not the same.

In the light of the moon-fired snow, the young black wolf lifted his muzzle to answer, to howl with a throaty fullness that could sail for miles. At last the tan wolf could sing side by side with the young black wolf in tones that tunneled up through time. She shaped her howl deep in her chest and let it braid together with his. The two wolves sang into the treetops, sang across the frozen lake, celebrating what they knew deep within their blood and in their bones.

Acknowledgments

I have so much gratitude to express, all straight from my heart: to Houghton Mifflin Harcourt editor Ann Rider, whose wisdom and grace made my experience so positive as *Summer of the Wolves* grew into its adulthood after a lingering adolescence. My readers helped me more than I can say with their many thoughtful questions and helpful catches: to Judith Bernie Strommen for her multiple readings over many years, her razor-sharp questions, and her belief in Nika as a character; to Beckie Prange and Consie and Roger Powell for their woods-wise insights; to Jess Edberg from the International Wolf Center, who sniffed out wolf facts for correctness; to Johnnie Hyde for her trust in me as an author and her support for this story; and to Claude and Laurel Riedel for their insights into child development and children seeking new families. I am grateful to Lisa Pekuri for her thorough, insightful proofreading; and to Juanita Havill for her many early manuscript readings, her warm encouragement, her professional knowledge and advice. Warm thanks to Jim and Judy Brandenburg for sharing the histories of our local wolves and for their encouragement and support; and to Judy for her eagle eye for facts and language. Heartfelt thanks to Steve Foss for his wonderful cover, a fine photo of a wild black wolf from our local forest. Many thanks to Marion Dane Bauer, Sandy Benitez, Susan Ray, and all of the Tuesday night writers for their encouragement as I began this book many years ago. It all started with Emile Buchwald's class and the commitment and time of Saturday-Morning-at-Ridgedale writers as we all began to write for children.

I am especially appreciative for the International Wolf Center and the excellent job they do teaching the world about wolves. Volunteering with the International Wolf Center and the Carlos Avery Game Farm allowed me unforgettable experiences up close with captive wolves and pups. My thanks, as well, to the many individual wolves with numbers and names who taught me so much: to wolves in my neighborhood who occasionally grace us with a glimpse; to Nyssa, Grizz, Maya, Aidan, and Denali, wolves from the IWC I have, in a small way, helped socialize, and who honored me with naps in my lap. A special thank you to my high school English teacher, Barbara Callender Olson, who showed me the joy of literature and planted a seed for my love of writing and a belief in myself. To all of my former students and the inspiration of sharing bits of their lives, to the Community of Ely, the inspiring people I have met there, and to its residents who live with wolves, struggling sometimes with the closeness yet benefiting from the wilderness that is their shared home. I thank my close friends, my husband Steve, and my children, Nick and Anna, for their patience when I have disappeared into my writing.

Finally, I am thankful for the memories of three strong women: my aunt, Charlotte Gill; my mother, Alice Mc-Near Carlson; and her dear friend Elinor Watson Bell, owner and lover of the actual Little Berry Island, where, as a child, I first set my foot in a northern wild place and fell in love.